For Nariece

PROLOGUE

MIRIAM

I'm the only one who gets out at Keston, the sight of the tiny station dragging my mood down with its emptiness. I linger to watch the train pull out from the platform, the whistle signalling the end of my adventure. I wish I hadn't said those things to Khaled, but I can't stand the thought of him going out with someone else. He says he's going to tell her, but will he really? I pick up my bag, the weight pulling down on my shoulder. I'm so glad I brought my bike.

Why did I promise I would tell Mum about him? She'll say he's too old, he's a different religion, and all those things that don't matter one bit, I know she will, but she doesn't know what he's like, how can she? My insides tingle every time I think back to last night – when he kissed me. It wasn't how I expected it to be, somehow I knew what to do when his soft lips pressed against mine.

My bike is there, where I left it; it's always a relief to see the familiar red frame chained to the fence, none of the wheels or other parts missing. I dump my bag into the wicker basket, glad to get the weight off my back. I rub my shoulders and stretch my arms before I bend down to undo the lock.

I hesitate at the path to the canal. Mum's told me never to go that way but it's so much quicker and it isn't dark yet. I pedal off extra fast so that I don't have time to change my mind.

It's getting chilly now and there aren't many people around. I pass a lady with a small dog and she smiles and stands to one side to let me pass. I feel better when she's there, but it only lasts a moment. I'm almost at the bridge when I hear a snap and my legs judder underneath me. I panic as my feet drop off the pedals and I realise the chain has come off. I swear out loud, then glance around quickly but there's nobody to hear me. I look up at the sky, it's starting to get dark, the wind is picking up and I feel a little afraid. My phone battery died on the train, just after I texted Helen. I quicken my pace, listening out for sounds. Why did I come this way? If Mum finds out she'll be mad at me for this and then I'll never be able to tell her about Khaled. I wouldn't be scared if he was with me now.

I walk as quickly as the bike will let me, my heart beating faster and faster as I start imagining all the terrible things that could happen. I swallow hard and focus on the light up ahead which I know is the lamppost on the bridge, marking the point where I will be able to get back on the road. There's a phone box up there and I'm going to call Mum and ask her to come and get me. It's properly dark now, it's taking longer than I thought but at last I've reached the bridge. I can see the phone box and I can hear the noise of a car coming. I rest my bike against the phone box and rummage around in my bag for some change, my hands shaking. Then I notice the broken glass, the receiver hanging, the wires sticking out at cruel angles. I'll dump my bike and pick it up tomorrow. I'm pulling my bag back over my shoulder when I notice the car. It's pulled into the side of the road, lights on, engine running, the door slamming as a man gets out. I know I mustn't speak to strangers, but it's dark and cold and I'm frightened. He might be able to help me.

He's coming towards me now, a big man, wearing a leather jacket and jeans. He stops and looks at my bike.

'What's the matter?' he asks, he has a rough London accent and a dark stubbly beard. I don't like him. He leans over the bike and I smell alcohol and sweat. I try not to wrinkle my nose.

'M... my bike... it's no problem, I'm almost home.' My voice sounds squeaky, I swallow hard, I don't want him to know I'm afraid.

'I'll give you a lift,' he offers, but it sounds like a command.

'No,' I say, remembering my manners, adding, 'thank you, but I haven't far to go.' It's true, although home seems far away and out of reach and I want so much to be there, right now. I edge away from the bike which I no longer care about. My heart is trying to bump out through my chest.

'I said I'll give you a lift,' he repeats, he sounds angry now. 'What's the matter with you Sadie?' He sways a little and his eyes are fierce as he grabs my shoulders, shaking me hard, his enormous hands hurting me, stopping me from telling him I'm not Sadie, really I'm not. I cry out and his face twists into a mask. He knocks against the bike causing it to fall against him and he starts to shout. I want to run, but my legs are rooted to the ground, his hands still digging into my shoulders, then he releases his grip and he is raising his large arm into the sky. I hope that my parents will forgive me as I see his arm flying towards me and I fall onto the cold hard ground.

CHAPTER 1

Sadie was pouting into the mirror, painting a shiny red bow onto her lips. She snapped her compact shut and put it carefully into her designer handbag. Now she was tapping on her Blackberry, shiny silver nails dancing rapidly over tiny pink buttons, tap, tap, tap. I wanted a phone exactly like hers. Suddenly Sadie whipped her head round and her deep green eyes fixed for a second onto mine. I looked away, furious. She mustn't recognise me. I scraped my chair back. I was out of here.

I didn't go far. The tree across the road was well placed to stand behind and I'd used it before. Like clockwork she exited the café, stopped to pat her hair in place then off she went, her dainty heels making tiny clicking noises on the pavement. She didn't notice me. She rarely did. Today she was wearing dusky blue skinny jeans, long drainpipe legs stretching giraffe like into expensive boots. She was expensive. People turned their heads to look at her when she passed by. She was that sort of girl.

Sadie was giving it some pace tonight. I had trouble keeping up. Skinny cow. The streets widened out as we got into a better part of town and there were more trees. Just before she stopped in front of the poshest house in the street a car horn sounded and a flash motor pulled up beside her. I was too far away to see who was driving. It wasn't her boyfriend's car. I memorised the number plate. She pushed her face through the driver's open window and pouted those ruby red lips. A masculine leather-jacketed arm reached out of the window and circled her waist, drawing her in. I wondered how that felt. Then she was in the passenger seat and being driven away from me. Damn! At least I'd got the car number plate.

I walked back through the town. I knew where she'd got her bag from; I'd seen them in the window of the boutique at the far end of the high street. A bell tinkled as I opened the door. Two sales assistants were chatting behind the counter, and neither of them looked up. A grungy looking girl was rifling through a pile of belts.

The bag was near the counter, on a shelf. I lifted it down, the leather felt soft and delicious. I opened the clasp and looked at the price tag. My breath caught as I saw the red line scratched through the price. It was still expensive, but I had my birthday money left. This bag would make me that little bit more like Sadie. I couldn't get it to the counter fast enough.

The house was dark as usual. Mum was at work. I sighed and flicked the hall light on. I pulled off my jacket and slung it over the bannister. I imagined Sadie doing the same with her chic red coat. She had a proper family; I bet she didn't rattle around that great big house when she got home.

9

I went into the living room and switched the lamp on. The leather sofa gleamed at me, the floorboards smelt of fresh polish. The cleaner must have been in. I held my breath as I extracted the bag from the smart carrier. It was gorgeous. Soft warm brown leather, with a large bronze buckle, clearly expensive. I stroked it lovingly, then put it over my shoulder, the way Sadie did. Perfect.

I wondered what Sadie was doing. I had imagined the scene so many times. The large open kitchen, the mum at the island in the middle fixing her some food, smiling at her, loving her. Today she was playing a game on her Apple Mac with her sister, her arm slung around her shoulder. I had no idea what it must feel like to have a brother or sister.

My phone rang. I grabbed at it, hoping it might be Tess. Mum. I pulled a face.

'Darling I'm still at work,' she said, in that breathless always in a hurry way she has. 'Are you alright to fix yourself something to eat?'

'You mean like I do most nights?'

'Oh please don't start Jasmine, you know I can't leave work early, much as I'd like to. How was school?'

I sighed. 'School was fine, mum. I'll get myself some food.'

'There's some pasta left in the fridge, you can have that.'

'Sure.'

'Good girl, I'll be back around nine, OK.'

Great. Another evening amusing myself. My phone buzzed. Mum again.

'Yes?'

'Have a think about what I said this morning. About the summer.'

'I've spent all day trying not to think about it,' I said, cutting her off.

My stomach was making little growling noises. I went into the kitchen and opened the fridge. I stared at the pitiful contents. Three bottles of wine shaded from pink to white, a square of cheese and the sad looking bowl of congealed pasta. I ignored the pasta, cut myself a slab of cheese and grabbed a bag of peanuts from the cupboard.

I slumped back onto the sofa and aimed the remote at the TV. It was almost time for *Crimewatch*. I love anything to do with crime, a complicated problem to solve. I'm good at finding things out. That's how I had started with Sadie, she was kind of an experiment – I didn't expect to become quite so good at it.

The wanted pictures were being lined up on screen now; this week's alternative top ten. The best bit. I like to imagine who these shady characters are, what kind of lives they lead. They always look well dodgy. The usual suspects flashed on the screen before me, hooded, bearded, tattooed, a woman with her hair scraped back and hard eyes. The last figure on the screen was completely different and made me drop the bowl of peanuts on the floor. This man had no hood, or beard, or tattoo, but I'd know his face anywhere. He was my dad and he was staring out of the television right at me.

11

CHAPTER 2

At that moment the front door banged and I heard Mum's voice.

'Jasmine, I'm home.' Damn. I scooped up the peanuts and zapped the screen to a different channel. Why did she have to turn up now? What was Michael supposed to have done? He didn't deserve to be called dad, I didn't even know him.

I heard doors slamming in the kitchen, the fridge opening and shutting, then Mum appeared in the doorway, a large glass of pale yellow wine in her hand.

'Jasmine, what is it? You look as if you've seen a ghost.'

She'd got that right.

'Jasmine?'

'I'm alright Mum, just a bit tired. Have you finished work now?'

'I've got a few emails to reply to. This new campaign is going to be massive.' Mum said that about every campaign. Although this was the first time she was being asked to go abroad.

'I want to talk to you before I start. Don't look like that, for goodness' sake, try and act your age.'

Yesterday morning Mum had blown my world apart.

She'd told me that the advertising agency she worked for were sending her on an important assignment in New York this summer and that I was going to have to go and stay with one of her friends. I hadn't spoken to her for the rest of the day.

'I don't want to stay with any of your friends. Why can't I stay here on my own? I'm old enough.'

'No you're not. I'd probably get reported to the press as one of those ghastly mothers who go off to Ibiza with a toy boy and leave their kids home alone.'

'You said it.'

'Jasmine!'

'Tess could come and stay.' My best friend Tess was staying with her elder brother Mark for the summer and I couldn't wait.

'I'm sorry Jasmine, but I can't leave you two girls on your own here. You're too young. I'll sort something out.' She swilled the liquid around in her glass, staring into it. 'Please don't make this difficult. Things aren't good at work, Jas. We're losing contracts and people are being made redundant. The truth is if I don't take this post in New York then I'm out of a job.'

'So why can't I come with you?'

She sighed. 'It's not appropriate. You know what I'm like when I'm working... and now that Gran is in the care home there isn't really any other option.'

I went off upstairs to my bedroom and lay down on my bed, thumping the pillow as hard as I could. I didn't like any of Mum's friends. Why couldn't I stay here with Tess? We could have a great time. I was so annoyed about the summer that I had almost forgotten seeing that familiar face on *Crimewatch* earlier . That same face that had walked out on Mum and me when I was a baby. Mum came home from work one day and Dad didn't; he was gone, just like that. I had hated him ever since.

I went outside onto the landing and leant over the bannister. There was no sign of Mum in the living room. She must be working, which meant she wouldn't notice anything that was going on around her. I had to find out what he was wanted for. I had been so shocked to see his picture that I hadn't taken in anything that the newsreader was saying.

I switched on the TV in my room. I had a large flat screen TV high up on the wall. Usually I sprawled out on the bed but today I was way too tense. I could barely sit down. I found the episode I wanted and fast-forwarded through to the part where he had appeared. There was no doubt in my mind; I was one hundred per cent certain that the man on the screen was my father. I had spent enough time as a child studying that face, looking for answers; I would know it anywhere.

My hands were shaking, I realised, as I started the recording a little earlier than necessary. Did I really want to know? Maybe I should turn the set off and forget I had ever seen it. Nobody else was going to recognise him, as long as Mum didn't get to see it and she hardly ever had time for television. But I knew that wasn't going to happen. I had to find out the truth. I turned up the volume.

My dad was number ten in the wanted gallery.

Last on our list this evening is this man who discovered the body of missing teenager Miriam Jackson. Miriam was found in undergrowth in a wood close to the village of Keston, Buckinghamshire. She had failed to return home as expected and was last seen on her way home from London on Sunday. The man, who had been out for an early morning jog, phoned the police from a nearby phone booth and waited until they arrived, but disappeared before officers had a chance to question him properly. His image was caught on a nearby CCTV camera as he came out of the phone booth and police are anxious to eliminate him from their inquiries. He is tall, white, of athletic build, with short dark hair and was wearing a black beanie hat, adidas shorts and a red t-shirt.'

My heart stopped as he appeared on the screen again.

'Anyone who recognises this man or has any information about this crime please call 0800...'

I pressed pause. My legs were now shaking alarmingly.

I had to take control of myself. I took some deep breaths. I was being ridiculous. Why didn't I get Mum up here now and show her the picture? Then she could tell me that I was wrong; how could I possibly recognise him from a photograph?

I didn't want to tell Mum. Here was the opportunity I'd always wanted, to find out the truth about my dad and if he was guilty, then I would be the one to find out.

CHAPTER 3

Next morning an urgent need for toast twisted around in my stomach, luring me downstairs. It would be nice to have the kind of mum who fixed breakfast in bed on a Saturday morning but mine didn't usually surface until midday at weekends. A pile of envelopes lay on the doormat. I picked them up. Three boring official looking letters addressed to Mrs C Robertson. I could never understand why Mum insisted on being called Mrs. I was never going to change my name. Everyone's parents are divorced these days. The *Crimewatch* image sprang back into my mind.

I was wearing one of Gran's jumpers. Gran used to knit me lovely jumpers before she went into the home. I didn't like thinking about Gran; last time I saw her she had asked me who I was.

I made myself some toast and jam plus a pot of tea and settled down on the sofa with my phone. I needed an accomplice and I knew exactly who to ask. Tess.

Tess and I had bonded on our first day at primary school at the back of a maths lesson, when Glenda Barrett had lost her pencil case and I had tracked it down to the stationery cupboard, announcing to the class that I had solved my first case as a wannabee

16

detective. Most of the class had avoided me after that, but Tess was undeterred. 'Quirky,' she called me now.

I texted her and told her to ring me immediately when she woke up. Seconds later my phone rang.

'I've been up ages,' she said. 'Mum's been hoovering outside my door for the past hour. I am about to kill her. What's up?'

'I think I saw Michael last night on television.'

'Michael?'

'My so called father.'

'What do you mean he was on television?'

'It's beyond complicated,' I said. 'I wish I didn't have to tell you over the phone.'

'The holidays will be here soon enough,' she said. 'I break up a week before you, remember. Only one week to go for me.'

'You won't believe what Mum's trying to make me do. She's got to work in New York and is trying to get me to stay with one of her friends. Can you imagine?'

I was trying to work out which of Mum's awful friends she would try and fob me off on. Esme was her best friend, she was OK but she lived with her boyfriend in a tiny flat in Hampstead and I didn't think she'd want me hanging around cramping her style. Clare was the obvious choice, but she was Mum's boss so I wasn't sure whether she would be going with her to New York. The worst-case scenario would be her friend Shona from her Pilates class; she was a health nut, a non-smoking teetotal vegan who never stopped talking about her latest fad.

'Jas! You can come and stay at Mark's!'

'Do you reckon? That would be amazing!' Tess had

17

moved away in year seven. Her father had got a job up north and within weeks of telling me, tears streaming down her face that she was leaving, she had gone. Her elder brother had recently moved back down here and I couldn't wait to spend the summer with her again, just like we used to.

'So come on, tell me about Michael.'

'OK, well you won't believe this but last night Michael's picture came up as one of the wanted people on *Crimewatch*. Apparently he found the body of a teenager but didn't wait around to give the police his name.'

I swear I heard her jaw drop open, like they say in books, I really did.

'OMG,' she said, 'you mean your dad – Michael – is wanted in relation to a murder?'

'He reported it,' I said, 'but whether he had anything to do with the actual crime...' Jeez! Were we really discussing a murder?

'It can't possibly be your dad,' she said, regaining her composure. 'For a start, how do you know what he looks like? Weren't you still a baby when he left?'

'Yes, but I've got all mum's photos of him – I took them before she could throw them away. I've got quite a few of his things. She doesn't know I've got them. She chucked most of his stuff out apart from a few things which she shoved in the loft. When I was about eight and curious to find out everything I possibly could about him, I went up there and had a look. The photo they showed on screen is identical to the one that I have. I'll email it to you later. He looks slightly older, but then he would do, wouldn't he?'

'Well it's easily sorted — when you show your mum the wanted picture she'll definitely know whether it's him or not.'

'Tess,' I hissed. 'Mum can never know about this. She'd report him straight away.'

'Well that's good isn't it?'

She didn't get it at all. 'Of course it isn't good, I don't want her interfering. I need to find out what he is up to.'

Tess went all serious.

'Jas,' she said gently, 'you don't know anything about this man. He might well be guilty.'

'I know, and if he is then I will have been right about him all along,' I said. 'But I need to know. I'm going to find out exactly what kind of person he is. And you are going to help me.'

CHAPTER 4

I stared at the now silent phone in my hand, wishing it would come back to life with Tess's voice. It was still early. Mum wasn't up and wouldn't be for hours. A boring Saturday morning stretched ahead of me. Unless... Saturday meant Sadie would be in the café in town. Somehow after following her the first time I was curious to see exactly how far I could go. It wasn't as if I had anything else to do. I grabbed my coat and headed out of the door.

She looked at me curiously when I walked in and I put my head down. I didn't want her to see my tomato cheeks. My heart was fluttering extra fast.

A peal of laughter made me look over at her table. Two of her friends had just come in. I was feeling a bit conspicuous. Usually I put my hair up under a cap so that she wouldn't recognise me, but I'd rushed out without thinking. My hair is scarlet red – the exact same colour as Sadie's. Her hair had been so different to mine and I'd started obsessing about whether it would suit me. I'd taken a photo to the hairdressers and they'd done a really good job matching the shade, and the style was pretty accurate too.

The two boys who had sat down with her were gazing at her from under their identical hair, swept forward into carefully arranged mops. Their t-shirts and jeans were like a uniform too. Sadie was so popular she made me sick. Her ruby lips were pouting and talking and the boys were hanging onto her every word. Every now and then she picked up her pink phone and tapped away, showing the screen to the boys and laughing. She had her bag at her side, my identical one was on the chair next to me. I hunched down into the armchair. A good detective does not get spotted.

I kept my head lowered but she was so engrossed with her admirers that there wasn't much danger of her noticing little old me in the corner. I sighed and looked around the café. The place was livening up now, there was a queue at the counter and the enormous pile of pastel coloured cupcakes had gone down loads since I had last looked. The baristas in their identical black t-shirts and aprons were darting about, conjuring up a hundred different varieties of coffee. Sadie always drank espressos and never ate cakes; she was obsessed with her weight. I couldn't be bothered with all that. I scooped up the crumbs from the remains of my cake and licked my fingers.

Sadie and her boys were leaving now. I had no intention of following her today, I was too conspicuous with my hair and bag. I switched on my laptop and opened it up. My Sadie file would distract me. I added the number plate that I had jotted down the other day. So far the facts I had accumulated were:

21

Sadie 17

St Helena's sixth form year 12 A levels Art French and History

Lives with mum dad sister Alicia 13 and brother Joshua 17

Boyfriend AJ, 20? Works as a fashion photographer. Drives a Porsche registration number T5XQ OLR

Best friend Madeleine

Drinks double espresso and vodka and diet coke

Smokes menthol cigarettes socially

Favourite designer Stella McCartney

My Sadie list was growing. The car the other day annoyed me. Who was the driver and what had happened to AJ? I clicked on Sadie's Facebook page. AJ was still listed as her boyfriend. I opened his picture just for the hell of it. Gorgeous, brown eyes and dark curly hair. Why would she cheat on him? I dragged myself away from AJ and added a description of the car. *Red sports car.* I googled it to get a name for it. Jeez, cars are boring but detail was crucial to being a good detective. AJ's Porsche was black and two years old – a gift from his dad when he upgraded his own car. I bet he didn't know about Mystery Man.

The tables around me were heaving now and a woman with an extremely loud voice was shouting into her phone. I wondered where Sadie was going on holiday – I was pretty sure about one thing – no way would she be expected to stay with one of her mum's sad friends for the summer.

I had first encountered Sadie in the public library in town. I'd done a double take at the sight of such an exotic specimen in the teen zone. Since the library had been done up, it wasn't such a sad place to hang out in. She was seated at the end terminal staring furiously at the screen. I went and sat down in the space next to her. I had my headphones on, but my music had come to an end. I moved my head around a little; let her think I wasn't paying attention to her.

A librarian was walking past with a pile of books and the girl had put her hand in the air and summoned her over.

'Can you help me?' she asked. Her voice was, as I expected, smooth and refined, a bit plummy. 'I'm trying to log into my email account and I can't remember my password.' The librarian gave her a curious look. 'It sounds like you need to set a new one. Make sure you choose something you can remember this time.'

The girl glared at her and typed something into the screen. After a few more minutes and a bit more tapping, she fished a pen out of her bag and jotted something down on an envelope that was lying on the table. It must have worked because after that she started typing furiously. I watched her out of the corner of my eye. Her hair was a brash, unnatural but wonderful shade of red, cut into a severe bob with the straightest fringe I had ever seen and her fingernails matched exactly. She was wearing gorgeous jeans and a black leather jacket. The jeans were Armani and her bag was one I recognised from a magazine. Envy filled

23

every pore of my body. At that moment, a stream of rap blasted from her bag. Now it was the librarian's turn to glare. Sadie looked at the screen to see who was calling and raised her beautifully neat eyebrows.

'Yeah?' she breathed, pouting at the screen. 'You're joking!' She stood up abruptly, pressed escape on the keyboard, grabbed hold of her bag and strode out of the door. I too grabbed hold of my jacket with one hand, picking up the envelope she had left on the table with the other. I hesitated for a moment, but this was too good an opportunity to practice at being a detective. I glanced at the front of the envelope before shoving it into my back pocket, grinning. *Hello Sadie Delaware*, I said to myself. Name and address, email log in details, not bad for a first meeting. I thought back to how I'd felt then, as I hurried after the retreating Sadie, who was tripping down the High Street, phone glued to her ear. Excited.

CHAPTER 5

Mum wanted to talk to me, I could tell. She was like an animal, poised for the kill.

I pretended to study the book balanced on my lap, sipping at my can of coke. I peeked at her out of the corner of my eye. My tall, oh so elegant mother. She was folded neatly behind her huge Apple Mac, all power suit and high heels. She didn't look like a mum. Real mums wore slippers and slopped about in jumpers and sweat pants. Mum hadn't been on that particular training course. Gran, on the other hand, was a proper gran with curly grey hair, flowery dresses and she worshipped her only granddaughter. She was actually Michael's mother, but had been so disgusted with Michael running off like he did that she had taken mum's side and had very little contact with him. I closed my eyes, trying to shut Gran out of my head. Why did I have to come from the smallest family ever? One girl in my class had seven brothers. I had asked Mum if we could have a pet once and she had suggested a goldfish. Really, a goldfish!

Mum filed a stray lock of hair behind her ear. Her head trembled slightly as her eyes flew back and forth, taking in the document on screen.

'I know you're not reading,' Mum said, swivelling her chair and resting her icy eyes on me.

'Am!' I said, staring hard at my book. Her stare was making me squirm. 'I'm surprised you noticed. Your work is usually far more important that anything I have to say.' She stood up from the chair and placed herself onto the sofa next to me.

'Look, I know you're angry with me but we need to sort this out. I'm sorry I sprung the New York trip on you, but Clare is happy for you to stay there so that's a weight off my mind.'

'Mum,' I groaned, 'I'm not staying with Clare. Jeremy's a creep.' I couldn't stand to look at Clare's son, let alone share a house with him.

'Oh don't be ridiculous. He's a perfectly nice boy, he's just a bit awkward around girls, that's all. It's his age.'

'Perfectly nice,' I mocked. 'He's a pervert.'

'Jasmine stop it. You're being deliberately difficult as usual.' I bit down on my lip to stop myself from exploding.

'I've got a better idea. Tess says I can stay with her at Mark's. He's twenty now, and you've always said how much you like him.'

She narrowed her eyes.

'He's really responsible, he's got his own flat and everything!'

'That's not a bad idea. Let me think about it. Now let me get on with my work.'

I headed off upstairs. Mum's bag was in the passage, the evening's paper sticking out. I took it up to my bedroom with me. I switched my iPod on and turned it up full blast. I'd rather scratch my own eyes out than stay with bossy Clare and creepy Jeremy.

I lay on the bed and unfolded the paper. Miriam Jackson was on page three. The now familiar picture leapt out at me. I scanned the article, eager to verify what Mum had told me. There it was. Miriam had disappeared at four o'clock on Friday May 26th. The day Mum had met Michael at the station. I opened my laptop and typed *map of Keston* into the search engine. A colourful square revealed itself bit by bit. I hovered the mouse over it. *Map of Keston, Buckinghamshire*. I froze on my bed. Mum had said Michael was living there. Amersham, that was it. I opened the map fully and moved it around over the screen. There! Amersham was right next to Keston. I sat back, the thought that it was perfectly possible that Michael had gone to Keston going round in my head. If Michael wanted to see me, this could be a perfect opportunity to find out exactly what he had been up to when Miriam disappeared.

CHAPTER 6

Pear Tree House was a series of connected low-level buildings that screamed institution from every brick. Curtain free windows revealed several seemingly empty bedrooms, with two large lounges, mostly full of old people. Rows of chairs faced a huge television screen, which had the volume turned up very loud. One old lady clutched a large clock face to her.

'Three o'clock dearie,' she said, tilting the clock towards me. I looked away.

I signed in, then scanned the faces quickly, most of the old people were asleep and there was no sign of Gran. She'd told me she preferred to stay in her room. That was before she'd forgotten who I was.

A nurse bustled towards me.

'Hello dear,' she said. 'Jasmine isn't it?' I nodded, hoping this smiley lady was looking after Gran. 'Margaret isn't so well today,' she said, 'she's getting frustrated that she can't remember things. Hopefully you'll be able to cheer her up.' My mood dropped a little. Gran's door was open and I could see her sitting in an armchair, gazing out of the window. She was holding something in her hand. I pulled a smile onto my face and went in.

'Gran,' I called quietly, not wanted to startle her. She turned her head slowly and gazed at my face. Suddenly a smiled made her face go all crinkly. 'I was hoping you'd come. Sit down and talk to me. I haven't spoken to anyone for days.'

I perched on the edge of the bed, unable to relax. 'It's me, Jasmine,' I said.

'I know dear. Have you been at school today?'

'No,' I said. 'It's Sunday, Gran.' The object on her lap was a photograph, a black and white one. She was clutching it tightly.

'You see there I go again, I don't know what day it is in here. Every day seems the same. Where am I anyway? Is this my house? I don't remember inviting all these people in. Its most peculiar.'

I sighed. 'It's where you live now Gran. It's very nice, lots of people to talk to and you've got your own room.'

She wasn't listening. She was staring at the photograph.

'Where is he? He said he would come and see me again.'

'Who, Gran?'

'Him, of course.' She held the photograph out for me to look at, but wouldn't let go of it. I peered at the couple standing in front of an old fashioned looking car. It was Mum and Michael. I wanted to grab it from her hands and burn the details into my brain. I'd never seen a picture of them looking happy together before.

'Michael,' she said. 'Where is he?' She started to rock

backwards and forwards, agitated. Unease spread through me.

'I don't know,' I babbled. 'I haven't seen him for a long time. Mum and Dad got divorced. Don't you remember?' I added, forgetting. *Duh Jasmine*.

Gran lifted her head away from the photograph and the look she gave me threw a chill right through me. 'You're a liar!' she said.

'Gran! Of course I'm not. How can you say that…?'

'He promised me. He stood right there and he promised. He said he would come back to see me.'

'When was that Gran? When did you see him?'

'The other day. Look.' She pointed to a glass of yellow tulips on the window sill. 'He brought me flowers. First time in years a man has given me flowers.' She laughed to herself. The flowers were fresh, the water clear. A piece of paper was tucked under the vase. I pulled it out. Gran was still chuckling. It was another photograph. I shoved it into my pocket.

'What else did he say, Gran?'

'He said he would be back as soon as he could but he wanted to bring her to see me. I told him no, never.'

'Who did he…?'

Gran cut me off mid-sentence. 'How dare you come here without permission? He never could keep a promise. Why did he let you come?'

'Gran, it's me Jasmine, please…'

'Oh I know who you are,' she said, nodding slowly. 'You look like her but I'm not that stupid.' Her voice had got loud and shrill and I could hear footsteps approaching along the corridor. I stood up. The smiley nurse was no longer smiling. 'Is everything alright in

30

here? What's the matter Margaret?'

'This girl says she's Jasmine. I know who she really is. He knows I don't want to see her. I told him. I told him not to bring her.'

The nurse shot me an apologetic glance. 'I think you'd better go. She gets confused easily. Just go downstairs to the office and wait for me there.'

I picked up my bag, my heart bursting. Gran had always been my rock.

'It's her. It's the other one. Get her out of here. Pretending to be Jasmine she is, how dare she?'

'Let me get you a cup of tea Margaret,' said the nurse. I made my way towards the door.

'Just because you look like her,' shouted Gran. 'You can't fool me.'

I turned and ran down the corridor. 'Where's Jasmine?' Gran was shouting, 'Let me see her!'

Her words followed me down the corridor, mocking me. I charged along, head down, not wanting anyone to see the tears prickling my eyes. I rushed into the nurses' staff room and shoved my hands over my ears. Who did Gran think I was?

I paced around the small airless room, trying to make sense of Gran's words. What other girl?

The nurse came back, hurrying down the corridor.

'You poor wee thing,' she said. She was holding Gran's photograph. She caught my glance. 'She threw this at me – it seemed to be upsetting her.'

'I'll look after it,' I said, snatching it from her grasp. 'It's my mum and dad,' I explained. 'I haven't seen this picture before. We don't see him anymore.' I slid it into my bag, before she could change her mind.

'Yes, she talked about him a lot when she first came in. He's her only son isn't he?' I nodded.

'He left when I was a baby.'

'Your mum told me. I was surprised when he turned up here the other day.' I stared at her.

'So he was here?'

'Oh yes. She seemed really happy to see him.'

I had to put my hand on the wall to steady myself. 'When was this?' I asked.

'A few days ago,' she said.

'Did you speak to him? Or Gran? Do you know what she was talking about, saying I was pretending to be me?'

She took my hands. Her eyes were soft. Mine were hard and my skin was prickling.

'Jasmine, love, your Gran isn't well. She forgets people and faces. She didn't mean anything by her comments, so try and ignore them. Maybe come with your Mum next time?'

I snatched my hands from hers and jumped up.

'No way,' I said. 'She hasn't got time for Gran. I'm the only one who ever has.'

I turned and hurried along the corridor, unable to stop the tears now. I stopped at the signing in and out book at reception and glanced over my shoulder. There wasn't a soul around. I flicked back to the page for the 25th May. There it was, Michael Robertson. I took out my phone and snapped a photograph of the page. He'd arrived at 1.45 and left at 2.30pm. I frowned. His address was listed as the Metropole Hotel, Bucks. Wiping my eyes with the back of my hand I turned back to the current page and signed out. Then I ran as fast as I could out of the building.

I ran and ran until I couldn't breathe and doubled over in the street. I checked my bag; the photograph was still there.

I went into a corner shop and bought a bottle of water, and then went into the park to sit down for a bit. I needed to think things through. I went back over Gran's words in my head. The other one? I shook my head. The nurse was probably right – she was getting confused. It was the first time she had seen Michael in years, after all. It was bound to muddle her up.

When I got home that evening I went straight into the kitchen and took out a cold can of coke. Mum was in her study working.

'Hi Jasmine,' she called out. 'I'm in here.' Papers were strewn all over the desk and she was punching furiously into a calculator. She pushed her glasses onto her head and picked up a large glass of red wine, which had smudges of pink lipstick on the side. 'You timed it perfectly,' she said, lifting some books from the chair next to her, motioning me to sit down.

'Tina from Pear Tree House phoned. She told me what happened. I'm sorry, darling; I wish you hadn't had to experience that.' She paused to take a gulp from her wine glass. 'But it links to some news I have for you. There's no easy way to tell you this, so I'll just spit it out. I've been in contact with your father.'

'What?' I spluttered.

'He phoned me. He'd found out about Gran being ill and he needed some documents from her. We arranged to meet.'

'So you've seen him?'

She nodded.

'He came to my office.'

'When was this?'

'A few days ago'

I felt as if ice had been poured into me. I stared at her. 'You mean you actually saw him and you didn't tell me?' *And he's wanted on Crimewatch* – I managed to stop myself blurting out the words. I shoved my hands under my thighs and squeezed hard.

'Look, I should have told you, I was going to but... I'm telling you now.' She sat up straight and put her hands on the desk.

'Actually, he wants to see you.'

The mouthful of coke I'd just taken hit the back of my throat and almost burst back out of my mouth, making me cough.

'Why now?'

'His family are relocating to England this summer, from France. I imagine it has something to do with him that.'

I felt hot all over, just thinking about him. Gran had eventually told me that Michael had left Mum for another woman. I didn't understand how he could abandon us like that. And now he had another family.

Mum picked up her wine glass. 'I don't think it's a good idea.'

'Mum! How can you say that? You can't make decisions like this without asking me.'

'You don't want to see him do you?'

I closed my eyes, feeling nauseous. 'I don't know what I think at the moment.'

Mum went out to the kitchen and came back holding a wine bottle. She poured the rich red liquid into her glass and took a large mouthful. I wondered what it would taste like. Would that calm me down?'

'I am so angry with your father. How dare he interfere like this? Margaret made it clear a long time ago she wanted nothing more to do with him and now that she's ill he is taking advantage of her. Sneaking over to see her like that.' She took another large gulp of her drink and sat down again.

'It was horrid, Mum, with Gran. She was OK at first, a bit snappy, but at least she knew who I was, then suddenly she changed and started accusing me of being someone else.'

'What exactly did she say?'

'She said she knew I was "the other one" and that *he* had promised not to bring her.'

A shadow crossed Mum's face. 'What is it Mum?' I asked. 'Do you know what she was talking about?'

She paused for a second, then shook her head. 'It doesn't mean anything. Gran doesn't know what she's saying any more. It's sad, I know, but you must try not to attach any meaning to her words. I'm so angry with your father, I've a good mind to ring him up and tell him exactly what I think.'

'I didn't know who Gran was talking about at first when she said that Michael had been. It was only when I saw his name written in the book that I believed her.' A thought occurred to me. 'When did you see Michael, what date?'

Mum went over to the side table and opened her diary.

'Friday, May 26th. He came to my office. He was on his way to the station to get a train to Amersham.'

'Amersham?'

'It's in Buckinghamshire. That's where he's moving to.'

'Mum,' I said, drawing the word out as I tried to make sense of all the jumbled thoughts in my head. 'I think I would like to meet Michael.'

She raised her eyebrows. 'Jasmine I don't think...'

'Let me speak to him at least.'

'OK.'

'And about the summer, please let me stay with Tess and Mark. I promise I'll check in with Clare while I'm there so she knows I'm OK, and maybe I could meet up with Michael then.' I was tripping over the words now, they were spilling out of my mouth of their own accord. 'You can ask him, can't you?' I crossed my fingers behind my back.

Mum looked perplexed. 'I don't understand you Jasmine, why this sudden urge to see your father?'

'I need some answers, Mum.'

She stared into her wine glass and sighed. 'That means I'll have to speak to him again.' She looked as if she had something nasty in her mouth. 'You realize he has another family now.' She looked directly into my eyes. 'It isn't going to be easy for you. He said he was on Skype, that's probably the best way to go about it.'

Mum was always on Skype. Tess and I had tried it a few times but had spent the whole time laughing at the sight of each other. I doubted whether Michael would have that effect on me.

I left Mum to get on with her work. I went to the fridge and studied the array of wine bottles lined up in the door. I glanced over my shoulder. Mum was on the phone now. The pink coloured one was half empty. The bottle was icy to touch. I poured myself a small glass and took it up to my room.

I typed out the address which had burned itself into my memory into Google maps. While I waited for the site to open I pulled the photograph out of my back pocket. It was a passport sized picture of a woman with dark skin and shoulder length black hair. I had never seen her before. I turned the small square over. The name Nora was written on the back. I took the other photograph out, deliberately not looking at the unfamiliar smiles of my parents and pushed them both into the box with all my other dad stuff under the bed. I turned my attention back to the computer. Did I really want to make contact? Hesitation only lasted for a second. I had to find out exactly who my dad was and what he was up to.

CHAPTER 7

'Don't tell me – you've got a homework project. Read as many newspapers as possible this weekend! You've forgotten the *Financial Times*.'

Our local newsagent thought he was hilarious. Irritating is how I would describe his stupid jokes. If there was a nearer shop, I'd be there. As it was, I gritted my teeth and pretended to smile as he packed a copy of each of this morning's papers into a carrier bag.

At home I spread the newspapers around the floor. The word MIRIAM was all over the front pages. I propped myself up onto my elbows and started to read.

The family of murdered teenager Miriam Jackson last night appealed to witnesses to come forward.

'There must be someone, somewhere, who saw her on the train from Marylebone.' Police confirmed that evidence from CCTV cameras at the station was being looked at. Miriam was described by her Headteacher from the local comprehensive in Keston as 'a delightful girl, who was popular and very gifted in drama. She will be missed by everyone at Keston school.'

Miriam, 15, had been spending the weekend at a drama school in London, where she had won a place on an acting course. All students on the weekend course were staying at the Travelodge, which is adjacent to the hotel. The girl who shared a room with Miriam said that she seemed to be enjoying the weekend, and they'd made plans to stay in touch.

Miriam had been due back in Keston on Sunday evening. She texted a friend to say she was leaving London Marylebone at 4.30pm. and although her bike was collected from Keston station, she never arrived at her destination. Buckinghamshire police received a phone call from a man at 7.30am the following morning saying that he had found the body of a young girl in a field. The police took the man's statement but, distracted by the arrival of an ambulance, he disappeared before the policeman could take down his details. The man was described as clean shaven, with short dark hair and blue eyes. He was wearing running clothes as he had been out for a morning run.

Police appealed once again for the unidentified male who reported the body being missing to come forward. Detective Inspector Andy Summerfield said, 'We would like to be able to eliminate this person from our enquiries.'

By the time I had read through everything that was written about Miriam the newsprint was wriggling like ants in front of my eyes. I closed my eyes and lay back on the floor.

I called up a map of England to see exactly where

Keston was. It was pretty near Amersham and less than thirty minutes from London on the train. I double-checked the date. Yes, it was the same date that Mum had met up with Michael. That was a bit of a coincidence.

I took Gran's photograph out of my bag and studied it again, before hiding it with my dad stash under the bed.

My stomach made an embarrassing growling noise. I went downstairs and peered in the fridge. There was a piece of pizza on a plate left over from the other day, so I ate that. The cheese was yummy and gooey and I realised I hadn't eaten since breakfast. I was going over in my mind what on earth I was going to say to Michael. What do you say to someone who walked out on you fifteen years ago? He wouldn't recognise me, obviously. I wandered over to the bookcase and took down the photograph album that Mum had kept when I was younger. There were no photos of Michael, a few of Mum and I together but the rest were all me. Gran had taken most of these photos. I turned to the pages when I was about ten. I was standing on a country gate, wearing cut off denim shorts and a green t-shirt with Minnie Mouse on it. My hair was in plaits and the sun was shining on me, making my hair look golden and interesting. I had freckles on my nose and a scowl on my face. I looked angry even then.

I put the album down and stood and looked at my fifteen year old face in the mirror. The freckles had all but disappeared, and my hair was no longer blonde but I had been dying it red for ages. 'Scarlet Power' was the shade it was supposed to be. It fell just below my shoulders. Naturally it was a kind of nondescript colour. It was pretty straight so it was no trouble to emulate Sadie's red bob, but my eyes were deep set and I hated them. Hers were large and her eyelashes were like thick spiders. I tried to imagine how I would look to someone seeing me for the first time. My stomach lurched. Was I really going to let my father into my life?

My phone buzzed. Facebook update. I clicked on the link and waited. And waited. I must speak to Mum about getting a new phone. This one was positively roman. I would be a much better detective with the right gear. It was a post from Sadie. My heart quickened. I hoped I hadn't missed anything while I was obsessing over Michael.

Loving my new Gucci shades. Thanks mum I love you...

There was a photo posted. I made it as big as I could. I wanted those glasses. I scrolled through the rest of her page. AJ was still listed as her boyfriend, and there was no mention of Mystery Man. I closed her page then set about finding those shades. It didn't take me long to find the exact same pair. £225. *Jeez.* Might as well go down town now and see if I could find anything similar.

Exactly one hour later I was outside Sadie's house, Gucci shades perched on my nose, cap on my head, hiding my distinctive hair. Now I had no birthday money left. I hadn't had a chance to check the shades in the mirror but they were good and big for a girl detective to hide behind, and I was wearing Mum's long black mac as dark clouds glowered overhead. I hoped I looked like an escaped celebrity.

I soon realised I wasn't alone. A man clad in leather was sitting astride a motorcycle along the street, slightly along from Sadie's house on the other side of the road. He was drumming his fingers on the handlebars. He was tall and stockily built. I wondered what he was doing. He appeared to be waiting for someone. He turned his head and caught my eye. I hesitated, then headed towards him. Close up he was much older than I had realised, with peppery stubble and dark shades covering his eyes.

'Yeah?' he asked, firing the word out like a bullet. I swallowed, then went for it.

'I don't suppose you know someone called Sadie, do you?' I babbled, 'only she invited me round and I can't remember what number she said she lived at.'

'Sadie?' he said and turned his head to face me. I could see my reflection in his glasses. He took his helmet off of the handle bar. 'Can't help you love,' he said and pulled the helmet over his face. He turned the ignition key and the bike roared away from the kerb, the pressure forcing me to stumble back onto the pavement. I watched as the bike disappeared round the corner. Funny that, as soon as I mentioned the name Sadie he had driven off. Why was he in such a hurry?

CHAPTER 8

It took me precisely three minutes to find out the name of Miriam's friend. Helen Branning. Either my detection skills were improving, or the internet just made things too damn easy. Miriam's school site had an extremely enlightening chat forum. Helen was in Year eight at Keston Secondary School and had been Miriam's best friend. Although Miriam was in year ten, they had met at the drama club they both attended on Saturdays. Her address was also mentioned on Facebook. Job done, I turned my attention to Sadie.

It crossed my mind that now that I had a real mystery to solve, I didn't need to use Sadie as a guinea pig any more. It had become a bit of a habit though. The first time I had logged into Sadie's email account was like unveiling a box of treasures. The best part was her fashion blog *SadieStyle* where she posted daily tips on what to wear. It didn't take me long to get hooked – choosing what to wear every day was such a pain.

Dressing like Sadie was pretty easy. I just followed the tips on her fashion blog.

Maybe next I'd learn how to get a boyfriend. I wondered who this Mystery Man was. He sure as hell wasn't AJ. Was he the leather man with the motorcycle?

The answer had to lie in Sadie's Facebook contacts.

I spent ages scrolling through her friends. Nothing there. I went back into her email account and spent the next hour reading any personal emails. My eyes were drying out and I was about to give up when I noticed a message from someone called 'T.' I hadn't noticed it before.

Hi Babe, don't forget I'm picking you up from your place at 4. Don't be late.

Nothing incriminating, but I checked the date. I was right! It was the day I had followed Sadie home from the café and first seen Mystery Man. I wrote down 'T' and the number plate I had for the car. Then I went further back into Sadie's emails. There was only one.

Happy Families! it said.

What did that mean? Sadie hadn't replied.
I sat back, tugging at my hair. I went back on to Facebook and searched through Sadie's contacts again. No Ts which would fit. I snapped the laptop shut and rubbed my eyes. How was I going to find out who he was?

I stroked the pink casing of my new phone. It was a deep crimson kind of pink, more of a raspberry than a blackberry. Mum had agreed to buy me a new phone and one hour later I was in the Phone Shop. Jason the phone man had tried his best to persuade me to buy a different kind of phone, but I had to have the exact same one as Sadie.

I practiced typing a few messages, positioning my fingers in the exact same way as Sadie. The tap tap sound made me feel good, closer to her.

A high tech ping made me jump and nearly drop the phone. Ping meant email. I hoped it was from Tess so that I could show off my new phone. The sender's email address jumped off the screen into my brain. michaelrobertson@hotmail.com. OMG! My hand was trembling as I pressed the button to open it. It was short and to the point.

Hi Jasmine, I'll be on Skype at 5pm today and every day this week until I hear from you. Can't wait, lots of love, Dad.

I looked at my watch. It was 4.30pm. I read the email again. And again. It definitely said five o'clock. I lay down on my bed and closed my eyes. I felt a bit panicky and took some deep breaths, like they did on Casualty. I could do with a handsome doctor coming to my rescue. I was actually going to speak to Michael.

At ten minutes to five I was logged on and waiting. There was no question of waiting another twenty-four hours. My heart would fail from anxiety. My face was cold, my hands clammy. Suddenly a little box lit up in the corner.

Michael is online. Connect with Michael?

I took a deep breath and clicked on 'Connect.' The screen flickered and I closed my eyes. When I opened them it felt like magic. Michael was on the screen looking at me. He looked surprised for a moment, then smiled. I stared back.

'Jasmine,' he said, 'It's really you isn't it?'

I nodded like an idiot. Thoughts were racing through my head: *Of course it's me. Not that you would know what I look like. When was it you last saw me? Oh yes, when I was a baby. I've changed quite a bit since then. I don't dribble as much anymore. You walked out and didn't come back*

45

How could I forget?

My insides felt like ice. Even without the beard the face looking back at me was definitely the one I'd seen on the television, and in numerous newspapers ever since. Why had nobody seen him? His eyes were the same shape as mine.

'Jasmine,' he burbled, 'I can see you're in shock. Caroline said it was alright to get in touch with you. I'd like to see you.'

Was I really going to do this? Images flashed through my head – Gran shouting, Mum crying, Miriam Jackson's picture staring out of the newspaper, haunting me. Who was this man? I had last seen him on Crimewatch.

'I'd like the chance to explain to you.'

'Whatever,' I said.

'The thing is, my partner – and I . . .' he hesitated for a moment, or was it the connection – 'we're in the process of relocating to England. We've been in France for the past month, staying with her family in Lille, and we're spending the last weekend in Paris before we leave, and we thought you might like to join us in Paris?' He paused again, running his tongue around his lips. He looked nervous. 'Have you ever been to Paris?'

I wanted to shake my head but I was frozen into position. *Partner? Paris?* He was speaking again, his voice less confident, speeded up. ' . . . so would you like to come with us? It would be easier if you met us over there on the Saturday. That's the 26th July. Then if you want you can come back to our new house after, although you might have had enough of us by then.' He laughed, he sounded nervous. 'Or you can come back to London and stay with your friend. Jess, isn't it?'

'Tess,' I muttered.

'You'll love it in Paris.' I rolled my eyes – what did he know about what I like?

'You can get a direct train from St Pancras, I'll meet you at the other end. I'll email you a timetable - you choose the train you want to get and I'll book the tickets for you. First class. My treat.' He stopped as if he'd run out of air, chewing at his lip. It gave me a jolt. I had that same annoying habit.

'We can't wait to see you,' he added. Big mistake. As far as I was concerned his new wife – Mum's replacement – was an insult and an inconvenience. I looked away.

'Well,' he said, running his fingers through his hair. I felt a huge pang of sadness and a shot of excitement at the same time, twisting my insides.

I refused to meet his eyes after that. I could feel his, however, boring into my head.

'Jasmine, look at me,' he said. My eyes were fixed on the keyboard. 'I've got so much to tell you, but not like this. I want to talk to you in person, not via a screen.' The image flickered in and out of focus. I adjusted the camera a little. I wasn't done with him yet. Was I slipping from his view too?

'I can't talk about it now Michael,' I said. 'I haven't got time. Email me the details about tickets and I'll let you know when I'm coming.' I paused. '*If* I'm coming,' I said and switched him off.

CHAPTER 9

My Skype encounter with Michael had made me feel worse than I did after cross-country on a Friday with Miss Meek. On waking I'd checked out the fridge. Two sausages were lurking at the back, alongside a large bottle of diet coke. I poured myself a glass and threw myself back onto the sofa. My phone pinged. Another email from Michael – *Subject: Eurostar times*. I swung my legs over the side of the sofa and padded back to the fridge. At that moment I heard Mum's key in the door.

'Jasmine are you home?' she called.

'In here,' I said.

'I'll be down in a minute,' she said, her feet clattering up the stairs. I quickly opened the email from Michael.

Hi Jasmine, it was good to speak to you earlier. Here are the train times for Saturday 26th July. Let me know when you want to come and I'll book the tickets for you. Michael

Mum's face looked sort of collapsed. She was still wearing her work suit, but had kicked her shoes off. She plonked herself down on the sofa next to me, bottle of wine in one hand, glass in the other. I held up my phone.

'Very nice,' she said. 'Is that the one you wanted?' I

nodded. I opened up Michael's email.

'Look at this.' She took the phone from me, picking up her glasses from the table and perching them on her nose.

'So he's not calling himself dad anymore?'

I shrugged. 'He stopped being my dad a long time ago.'

'So you spoke to him earlier? How was that?'

'Well how do you think? It was weird. Skype is weird.'

'Do you want to see him?'

'I think so,' I said, 'I'm so curious that I kind of feel I have to.'

'Are you going to do something about this strange hair colour before you go?'

She picked up a tress of my hair and I pushed her hand away.

'Don't start about my hair, I'm not in the mood. Michael said if I choose the train time then he'll book the tickets for me. First class.' I snorted. 'As if that will make me forget everything just like that. He mentioned *her* as well. I'm not going to speak to her, I'll just pretend she's not there.'

'It was your choice to go and see him Jasmine. You'll have to make an effort, otherwise you'll have a horrible time and I'll spend my two weeks in New York worrying about you.' I gave her a look.

'Really? I thought you couldn't wait to see the back of me.'

'Don't be ridiculous. I don't choose to be at work so much, you know.' She poured herself another glass of wine. 'If I gave up work and went on benefits you

49

wouldn't be sat there with that nice new phone in your hand. You wouldn't like that one bit.'

She didn't get it all. She has no idea what I want and I couldn't possibly tell her.

'Which train shall I choose? It takes less than three hours. Not far if I change my mind.'

'Jasmine. You have to take this seriously. You cannot run away.'

'Chill out Mum, I'm only joking. Help me with this.'

Mum got out her laptop and we had a look at the Eurostar timetable. Despite myself, I felt a flicker of excitement.

All I knew about Paris was what I'd learnt from my school text book; French people ate strange food like frogs legs and snails, French women are always chic and fashionable and wear Chanel perfume. I'd heard of the Eiffel Tower, but then of course, so has everyone.

'Where did I leave my bag?' Mum asked, her eyes fixed on the screen as her fingers tapped.

'I'll see if it's in the hall.'

Mum's bag was abandoned on the floor. I took out the newspaper and glanced at the front page. A heading caught my eye:

Miriam Jackson breakthrough see page 5

I spread the newspaper out on the hall table and quickly turned to page five. At least the photograph of Michael had stopped appearing in the paper every time the case was mentioned. For once I was pleased that Mum inhabited a different reality from me most of the time and hadn't spotted it.

The thirteen-year-old best friend of Miriam Jackson has now told officers that fifteen year old Miriam was going out with a boy she had met online. Police are investigating the possibility that she had met up with him during the weekend drama course in London. While staying at the nearby Travelodge, Miriam had shared a room with a fifteen year old girl from Camden, who when interviewed knew nothing about the boy in question. Miriam's mother, Sue Jackson, 35 said that Miriam had never shown any interest in boys. Police are asking for anyone who knows anything about the boyfriend to come forward.

'Jasmine! What are you doing out there? Where's my bag?'

'Jeez!' I muttered to myself, gathering up the newspaper and folding it back together.

Back in my room, which I now thought of as my Detection Zone, I flicked through the comments from students at Miriam's school. Miriam had been sharing a room with a Fiona Barton, fifteen, from Camden. The name Fiona Barton fizzed and sparked in my head. Of course! Unwelcome memories of primary school flooded into my mind. A skinny eight year old with long white blonde hair, leader of the Girl Gang, who controlled the playground at Park Primary. I had spent most lunchtimes hiding up a tree while Fiona tempted the gang with promises of toffees for the first one to find me and bring me to her. Tess had kept in touch with her when she'd moved away – Tess was good like that, or deranged, as I preferred to think of her. Whatever she was, I was glad of it now, as she was going to have to reunite me with the leader of the Girl Gang. I tried hard to convince myself that she wouldn't remember me.

CHAPTER 10

'So remind me again where we're going?' Tess was sitting opposite me, her feet up on the seat next to mine. The train rumbled along comfortingly. I had a few days to spend with Tess before I had to go off to Paris. I couldn't believe she was finally here; it seemed like ages since we'd spent some proper time together.

'Keston,' I said, 'it's a tiny village near Amersham.'

'And the reason is…?'

'I'm investigating and you're my map-reader. Michael is buying a house in this area, which gives him a reason for being in this part of England. I want to see exactly where Miriam lived.'

Tess shook her head, her pale blonde curls bouncing up and down. Today she was wearing a floaty yellow dress and DM boots, with lots of silver bangles jingling around her arms.

'I must be mad. This is what my mum would call a Wild Goose Chase.'

I leaned against the window, watching the fields fly by. Sheep dotted my vision, then vanished, cows and haystacks taking their place. Not a goose in sight. The sky was blue and the sun was shining into my eyes, deflected by my Gucci shades.

'So tell me why you're even speaking to Fiona Barton,' I said. 'I'd just like to remind you that she terrorised me at primary school.'

'I remember you climbing that tree every day. I never told on you, you know.'

'Gee thanks. That makes it even worse. You know what she's like.'

'She went to the same Art Club with me at the Youth Centre. She was at a different secondary then. We weren't friends exactly, but I stayed in touch with her when I moved. We're only Facebook friends now. Why do you want to know?'

I handed Tess the newspaper cutting. She took her time reading it, her hair coiling down over her face. At the end of it she whistled. 'She certainly likes acting so it could be her. She still loves to be the centre of attention. She played Dorothy in *The Wizard of Oz* last year in her school play. She made sure that was all over her Facebook page so that she could show off about Khaled.'

'Khaled?'

'Khaled Hussein. Her boyfriend. He was the Cowardly Lion. They got together on the last night. Khaled plays in Mark's band so he knows them both quite well. Mark still asks about you.' She winked. I ignored her.

'Where does she live now?'

'Over in Marigold close. The posh bit.' That got my attention. The posh bit was where Sadie lived.

'Wait till you see Mark's flat. It's so cool that your mum says you can stay with us.'

'If she'd sent me to stay with Clare I'd have

54

reported her to the authorities.'

'You prefer Mark to Jeremy eh?' Tess poked me with her foot. I ignored her comment.

'Do you think you can arrange for me to meet her?'

'No probs. Now shut up and let me have a kip.'

I spent the rest of the journey looking out of the window, seeing nothing, everything going round in my head, along with the rhythm of the train. 'Michael, Sadie, Miriam, Michael, Sadie...' Tess dozed; head lolling back, mouth half open. It was a relief when we arrived, stepping out into one of those picturesque old stations that you usually only see on jigsaw puzzles.

I rummaged in my bag and handed Tess the map. She'd been a Girl Guide and was much better than me at that kind of stuff.

'So tell me exactly what we're doing,' she said.

'First we're going to find the school where Miriam Jackson went. It's marked here, look.' I pointed to the arrows and letters I had drawn onto the map. A large S marked the school and an H marked the house. My methods were advanced. 'Then we'll walk from there to her friend Helen Brown's house. I just want to see how far everything is from the station.'

Tess rolled her eyes. 'It's not very scientific, this, is it?'

'Shut up,' I said, 'Now which way do we go?'

Tess led me off down a long winding street, which eventually led into a village. It was completely unlike London.

'I think we've walked into a postcard!' Tess said. 'It's so quiet.' She was right. The only sounds were birdsong and an occasional car in the distance.

'Here we are,' Tess pointed. A sign to the left read *Keston School* and we took the turning, forced into single file. It was a proper country lane, but there wasn't much traffic to worry us, as we kept close to the side of the road, facing oncoming traffic as instructed by Tess.

'I've never been anywhere like this before,' she said. 'Where would you go shopping?'

'Exactly,' I said, 'I wonder if Amersham is like this too.'

'Is that where your dad lives?' asked Tess.

I nodded.

'You don't expect this kind of thing to happen in a quiet country place like this do you?'

'I know what you mean. In dirty old London, which is full of weirdos and druggies, maybe, but...?'

'Hey, do you think we need to be careful? The killer might be lurking behind a bush, following us right now.'

I glanced quickly behind me but the road was empty.

'Tess! Don't say things like that.' I shuddered, remembering the photographs from the newspaper, then Michael's face flashed into my head. Surely he couldn't be a murderer?

After that we walked in silence until we reached the school. It was not unlike Park Primary where Tess and I had met, a lifetime ago now. It was funny to think how we used to spend all our time together.

'OK,' said Tess, 'Follow me.' She studied the map for a moment. 'Yeah, this way. It's not that far.' She put Her hand on her hip. 'A good detective would time

56

how long it took to walk from the station. What do you think?'

I set the timer on my phone and we headed off, imagining the girl on the bike who never made it home from the station. I couldn't see Michael coming here – why would he? There was nothing much to do. It didn't look like the kind of place you pass through, it was a bit off the beaten track for that.

About twenty minutes later we arrived in a cul-de-sac; a row of identical houses curved into an arch.

'We're looking for number twelve,' said Tess, then pointed, 'I think that's it over there.' I followed her finger to the house on the end with a blue front door. I switched off the timer on my phone. 'Seventeen minutes and twenty seconds,' I noted. Tess turned to me.

'So we know how far it is. What now?' she said.

Good question. We were standing staring at the house when the front door opened and a woman came down the drive. She looked just like the picture of Helen's mum I'd seen on Facebook, only fatter, with darker hair.

'Can I help you?' she asked. She was wearing an apron and holding a dustpan and brush. She shielded her eyes against the sun with her hand as she came towards us.

'Let's run!' muttered Tess. I stepped forward.

'Hello,' I said, 'I'm Jane and this is my cousin Tania. We were looking for Helen.' The woman squinted at me, suspicious, her eyes lingering on the map in Tess's hand.

'You're not from round here are you? How do you

know Helen?'

'We're friends on Facebook,' I said quickly. 'When I heard about what happened — with her friend — I wanted to come and see if she was alright. She said it would be OK...' my voice drifted off at the sight of a girl in the doorway. Helen.

'Who is it Auntie?' Her clear voice rang through the air.

Helen's aunt stepped closer, speaking quickly.

'Her mother is away so I'm looking after her at the moment. She's been through a hard time. If she doesn't want to see you then you'll have to leave.' I nodded, glancing at Tess. She looked terrified. The woman turned and walked back to Helen. 'Some friends are here to see you,' she said. Helen looked over in our direction.

'Jas!' Tess hissed at me. 'What are you doing?' She motioned with her head for us to go. I turned away from her and followed Helen's aunt. Helen was watching me curiously. She was a slight girl with long dark hair and was holding a kitten in her arms. She looked at me quizzically for a moment then turned to her aunt.

'Can we have some juice please auntie? We'll go out into the garden.' She led the way through the house and I followed, aware of Tess's bangles jangling as she shuffled behind to catch me up. Helen went over to a table, covered with a flowery cloth. A jug of orange juice, a plate of biscuits and a Harry Potter paperback lay open face down on the table. 'Sit down,' she said, motioning towards some white plastic chairs. 'I haven'tgot a clue who you are but I'm bored out of my head. So now you can tell me exactly what you're doing here and why you just lied to my aunt.'

CHAPTER 11

'What do you mean?' My heart was thumping in my chest. Tess focused her attention onto the biscuits, avoiding Helen's eyes.

'I'm not on Facebook, so we can't be friends.' She avoided our eyes. 'Mum won't let me.'

'How old are you Helen?' asked Tess. Helen looked quite young and her voice was high and girlish.

'I'm twelve,' she said, 'in two months and three weeks' time I will be a teenager. I can't wait. Mum won't be able to stop me doing what I want, then.' Helen narrowed her eyes. 'So why are you here?'

'Look,' I said. 'Are you the Helen Brown who's been in the newspapers, the friend of that girl who disappeared?'

'Miriam,' she said, her lip trembling.

'I want to talk to you. I thought I had made friends with you on Facebook — I must have got the wrong Helen. It's a common enough name. When you do join Facebook then we can be friends for real.'

Tess raised her eyebrows. I nudged her under the table.

'It must be really hard for you, what happened to Miriam. I would hate it if anything happened to Tess.'

'Tess?' Helen looked confused. 'Don't you mean Tania?'

I held my breath for a moment.

'Look, I'm going to be honest with you OK? I'm Jasmine, this is Tess, from London. Well, I am, but Tess – oh never mind all that, it isn't important. We didn't expect to see your aunt like that; I didn't know what to say so I made up names on the spur of the moment. Everything else is true.'

Helen closed her eyes, clenching and unclenching her fingers. After a moment she opened her eyes and stared at me.

'What do you want?'

'Tess is friends with a girl called Fiona Barton. She's the one who went on that drama weekend in London and ended up sharing a room with Miriam. Tess's older brother Mark is best friends with Khaled. . . '

Helen gasped, her face going pale. 'Khaled?' she whispered and put her hand to her mouth.

I nodded slowly, looking at Tess for support.

'What's the matter? Do you know him?'

Helen shook her head, her lips pressed tightly together. There was a hammering sound in my brain.

'You must feel pretty lonely,' I said. 'I bet you haven't told anybody about this, have you?'

She shook her head. 'I can't. Miriam made me promise. I already feel bad about what I said to that policewoman, but Mum kept on at me and I was worried about Miriam. Do you think it's my fault that she…' her lip started quivering and her words dried up.

'Of course it isn't,' said Tess. She moved closer to Helen and handed her a tissue.

'It must be terrible carrying all these secrets inside of you, on your own,' I persisted. Tess threw me a warning look, but I ignored it. 'Wouldn't you feel better if you could tell somebody?'

Helen sighed. 'You promise you won't tell? I don't want to get into trouble.'

'I promise. We're on Miriam's side, remember? Together we might be able to help her.'

Helen glanced over at the house, then leant forward.

'I think you know anyway,' she said. 'It's Khaled, he's Miriam's secret boyfriend. The one she met online. I had to tell in the end, but I didn't give them his name. I pretended I didn't know. Then I saw it in all the newspapers and I thought if I didn't tell anyone his name then I wasn't betraying Miriam. That way I was keeping some of the secret, wasn't I?' Her eyes looked beseechingly at me.

'But Khaled can't be...' Tess started to say.

'Of course you were,' I said loudly, reassuring her, drowning out Tess's voice. 'But we didn't know. Khaled has never mentioned Miriam. So you don't have to worry about that, he isn't going round telling people and if you haven't told anyone then her secret is safe.'

'I've told two,' she pointed out sulkily.

'You can trust us,' I said. 'I promise on Tess's life.'

'Great. Thanks a bunch,' said Tess. At that moment Helen's aunt came to the back door and called her over. She ran back into the house.

'On my life!' said Tess. 'I might as well slit my throat now.'

'Don't be such an idiot! I can't believe you nearly told her about Khaled.'

'But he's Fiona's boyfriend.'

'Yes but she doesn't know that does she? And she doesn't need to know. We're not doing anything wrong and I've found out a crucial piece of information.'

'Crucial? How?'

'Well I don't know, but I'm sure everything will eventually fall into place.'

Tess shook her head. 'You're crazy. I should never have come.'

Helen appeared at the table at that point.

'Auntie Lou says you've got to go. She's taking me to the dentist's. Will you stay in touch with me?'

'Sure,' I said. 'Anytime. Do you have a mobile?' She recited the number slowly and I punched it into my phone. 'I'll ring you tomorrow. I promise. Come on Tess. Stop eating those biscuits.'

Helen led the way back to the house.

'You need to be careful,' Tess warned, as we walked back down the drive. 'She seems so young.' We turned back to wave. 'Are you really going to ring her?'

I looked back at Helen. She looked lost. Tess was right.

'Yes, I will.'

Suddenly it seemed terribly important to find out what had happened to Miriam, regardless of Michael and his involvement.

CHAPTER 12

The postman stepped back as I wrenched the door open.

'Easy!'

'Sorry, I didn't mean to make you jump.' I held out my hand. 'I think those are for me.'

He pushed his glasses up his nose, peering at the envelopes he held in his hand. 'Miss Jasmine Robertson.'

'That's me!' I said, grabbing it from him. It was slightly thick. My heart rate increased.

'Birthday is it?'

'Something like that.' I pushed the door shut with my foot, while trying to see through the envelope. It was the Eurostar tickets. It was really happening. I sat back down at the kitchen table where I'd left my breakfast when I'd seen the postman approaching. I took a large bite of toast and tried to swallow the anxiety I suddenly felt.

It was already getting dark when I left school after my revision class and set off to meet Tess, shivering as I stepped out into the windy street. She'd sent me a text at lunchtime. A light rain had started and I hurried around the corner to where I had arranged to meet her. Five o'clock her text had said. I wondered whether she'd seen Fiona. It was five minutes past and I was getting irritated when she suddenly appeared at my side.

'Let's go,' she said.

'Where are we going?' I asked.

'You wanted to see Fiona didn't you?' I stared at her. 'Come on,' she urged, pulling my arm. 'In here.' She dragged me into the door of a small café next to the bus stop. It was normally full of workmen and I had never been inside before. Sadie wouldn't be seen dead in a place like this. I looked around and there at a table at the back was Fiona. She was hard not to miss, with her icy blonde, iron straight hair and her thick black eye make-up. She was with a boy. A boy with short black hair and big brown eyes.

'Tess!' I hissed. 'Is that…?' She nodded. Khaled had his arm slung around Fiona's shoulders and they were looking at a newspaper, which was spread out on the table.

'Hi Fiona, hi Khaled,' she said. 'Do you remember Jasmine?'

Fiona raised her heavy dark eyes and stared at me. Her eyes flashed with recognition as her gaze travelled up and down. Her lip curled.

'You haven't changed,' she said.

'I hope you have.'

Khaled nodded at me. Tess pulled out a chair and sat down so I did the same. Although the paper was upside down I couldn't help noticing the headline *MIRIAM LATEST*.

'I still can't believe this,' Fiona said, pointing at the large black letters. She was very small and had dainty features, like a doll, which made her eyes stand out in a startling way. Khaled squeezed her arm.

'Fiona was sharing a room with Miriam, you know the girl who was killed?' Tess looked at me. I nodded.

'What is she doing here?' Fiona addressed the remark to Tess.

'Jasmine wants to talk to you about Miriam.' Khaled shifted around in his seat, he looked uncomfortable.

'I went to see Helen,' I said, 'Miriam's friend, Helen.' Tess shot me a glance. Something flickered across Fiona's eyes.

'So why don't you speak to her then, if you're so interested?'

'I have, she told me to talk to you.' My hands were starting to sweat; I was making this up as I went along. 'She feels bad for dropping you in it.'

'So she should.' Khaled's voice was deep, with a slight northern accent.

'A girl has died!' said Tess. 'She did what she had to.'

Fiona put her hand to her mouth. 'Yeah, you're right. I can't stop thinking about it.'

'What was Miriam like?' I asked Fiona.

'She was very funny. A great mimic. Some of the people on the course took themselves really seriously and she hated that.'

'It said in the paper she had a boyfriend. Is that true?'

Fiona nodded. 'She kept it secret for ages, but she had to tell me in the end because she needed me to cover for her when she went out in the evening.'

'Where did she go?'

She shrugged. 'I don't know. Out with her boyfriend

Does it matter?'

'So did you meet him?' I was watching Khaled out of the corner of my eye during this. He was playing with a sugar packet, twisting it round and round.

She shook her head. 'It was funny though, because when she went to meet him she was so excited and then when she came back her mood had completely changed. She wouldn't talk about what had happened and I hardly knew her anyway, so I didn't push it. She did say one thing.' She paused and took a sip of her coke. Khaled twisted the sugar again, tearing the paper so that it spilled out over the table. 'Clumsy!' she said, brushing it away absentmindedly.

'What was that?' asked Tess.

'She said she had wished she lived in London, how it was easy to escape here.'

'You mean she wanted to run away? You should tell the police.' That was Tess. Khaled's head shot up. His leg was fidgeting under the table.

'No, I think she meant it was easier to be anonymous here, to get lost among the crowds. I got the impression her parents were very strict, that she didn't have much freedom. She had a hard time even getting them to let her come on the course! She comes from a very small place, where everybody knows each other's business.' She rounded on Khaled. 'What? I've told the police all this anyway. I'd do anything to help them. It's awful, to think that she's... not here anymore.'

The woman behind the counter was counting out the cash in the till. We gathered up our stuff and went outside. The conversation continued on the doorstep.

'So is it true that she told you her boyfriend was a Muslim?' Tess persisted. Khaled rounded on Tess.

'What's with all the questions man? She's told you already. You're too nosy Tess, that's your trouble. Anyway...' he smiled down at Fiona. 'Muslim boys are the best innit?' He bent down and kissed her on the side of her mouth. 'Let's go babe,' he said. 'Tell Mark I'll see him tomorrow.' That was directed at Tess. He ignored me. He turned to walk off and collided with a girl who was walking past.

'Khaled!' she cried and threw her arms around him. Fiona narrowed her eyes and put her arm through his, pulling him possessively towards her. My heart started beating fast. I would recognise that red hair anywhere. Good job I had my hair up today and was still in uniform. Why exactly had I wanted to look like her? I kept my head down, making sure to keep them in view.

'Sadie,' he said, sounding confused.

'Let's go,' said Tess.

'Wait!' I hissed, grabbing her arm. I couldn't believe it. Khaled knew Sadie.

'What?' She shook my arm off.

'That girl with Khaled, do you know her?'

Tess looked ahead at them. Khaled and Sadie were engaged in conversation while Fiona pouted at their side, still clinging on to Khaled's arm. Sadie was different somehow. She wasn't flirting I realised. The hug had seemed almost needy.

'Oh her,' she said dismissively. 'She's one of those rich kids who live up by Blossom Hill. Mark knows her; he went to a party at her house once. You know those massive houses? He said it was a great party but he doesn't like her much. Says she's stuck up.'

'How does he know her?'

'He goes to college with her brother, Josh. He's alright, he comes round to our house sometimes to jam with Mark. Mark's thinking of asking him to join his band. Why do you want to know anyway?'

'I want to know everything there is to know about Khaled,' I said, 'since I found out about him and Miriam. He looked uncomfortable when you were asking Fiona about Miriam, did you notice? He's of far more interest to me than Fiona now.'

'Fallen for those big brown eyes have you?'

'Get lost!' I looked back over at Khaled. 'It looks like he's got a big enough fan club as it is without me joining in.' The group was breaking up now, going their separate ways. I watched as Sadie left. What was her relationship with Khaled? It bothered me. 'Let's go,' I said, my stomach in knots. Following Sadie was a crazy thing to do, and the realization that it had to stop struck me like a punch in my gut. Tess's phone bleeped in her pocket. She pulled it out.

'Fiona,' she said, 'that was quick.' She read aloud:

Did you see that cow with Khaled?!! BTW Jasmine's not as annoying as I remember.

'Gee thanks,' I said. 'I love her too.'

CHAPTER 13

The noise was still ringing in my ears. First the bell, the last bell of another year, next the scraping of chairs, thuds of doors slamming, followed by the thundering of hundreds of feet haring down corridors and escaping out into six weeks of freedom. Screaming and yelling the whole way. Even though I was now safely cocooned in the silence of the charity shop, my head hadn't quite recovered. I'd been volunteering here for a few weeks now – Mum's idea. I think she just wanted to get rid of me. Actually, I quite liked it but I wasn't going to tell her that. It wasn't all batty old ladies and creepy clothes as I'd imagined. The shop was in the posh end of town and some of the stuff was really cool. That Mary Portas woman would be well impressed. I had picked out some choice items for myself, designer gear, new with tags, far too good for a charity shop. The volunteer in charge on Fridays was so old – when she wasn't making tea she was nodding off out the back, so I could pretty much do as I liked.

Today Gladys was putting her feet up in the stockroom so I was working on the till. I was making some notes on my phone; trying to make sense of the information I had learnt over the past few days. I wrote down a list of names, *Miriam, Helen, Fiona, Khaled*. I hesitated, added *Sadie*. Crossed her off. Thinking about Sadie made me squirm. She knew Khaled, so what? She had no connection to the case. Then I wrote down Thursday 25th and Friday 26th May. I drew up a timetable of Michael's activities. I had him visiting Gran on Thursday and staying at the hotel. On Friday he'd gone to meet Mum. Was he travelling back to Amersham? Or France? What had he done on Wednesday evening? I thought about the photograph. Maybe Nora was his girlfriend: I wouldn't put it past him. A cough startled me. A lady with a terrifying hairstyle stood at the till, holding out a blue handbag and a ten pound note. I checked the tag.

'Five pounds please,' I said, taking her money and giving her the change, stifling a yawn. As she opened the door to leave she held it open for a customer. A blonde girl wearing my school uniform came in. Fiona. What was she doing here? She came over to the counter, her eyes travelling to the door behind her before. She wrinkled her nose.

'It not as smelly as I expected.'

The shop was empty. I glanced towards the back. There was no sign of Gladys.

'Tess told me where to find you.' She glared at me. I glared back. Dark shadows under her eyes made her look washed out.

'Did you want something?' I asked.

'How well do you know Helen?'

'Pretty well.'

'You're a liar,' she said, stepping closer into my space. 'I spoke to Helen last night. She told me all about your visit . What are you playing at? What's all

71

this to you anyway? I don't get it.'

Her voice was loud now, causing Gladys to stick her head out of the stockroom.

'Is everything alright dear?' I made a snap decision. 'Could you look after the till for a bit, Gladys?' I asked, 'I need to speak to…' I hesitated for a second. '…my friend for a minute. I won't be long, I promise.'

'Of course, dear.' She shuffled over to the counter, smiling. 'You go out the back; I'll keep an eye on the till.' She patted Fiona on the arm. 'Boyfriend trouble, I expect.' Fiona shook Gladys's hand away and I led her over to the stockroom. There were a couple of chairs in there and I lifted a pile of jigsaw puzzles off one and dumped them on the floor.

'Sit here.' I said. Her eyes looked red.

'Has Helen said anything to you about Miriam's boyfriend?' she asked.

Now I knew how a mouse in a trap felt. 'A bit,' I said.

'Stop lying,' she said. 'I know what she told you 'cos she told me too. About Khaled.' She burst into tears. I rummaged in my pocket and pulled out a scrunched up tissue, but she batted it away. 'It doesn't matter,' she said. 'He dumped me last night, before Helen rang. We had a huge row after we left you, about that Sadie cow. She's after him, I know she is, but he can't see it. Anyway he said I was too possessive and he couldn't handle it anymore and that he'd had enough.' She wiped her eyes with her hand and sniffed. 'The thing is, it hadn't been right between us for some time, but now I find out he's been two-timing me I just feel so humiliated.'

'Don't be,' I said. 'It's probably for the best.' I held out the tissue again and this time she took it and blew her nose loudly.

'Helen told me she had no idea who you were when you turned up at her house. Why are you interested? What's it to you? I don't get it.'

She'd put me on the spot; no way could I tell her about Michael. I shrugged. 'I was playing at being a detective. A girl our age getting murdered like that, it makes you think, you know? As Tess knew you and there was a bit of a connection to Helen, I wanted to see what I could find out. Maybe I shouldn't have . . .' I shrugged. Why was everyone getting so bothered about me talking to Helen? It was part of my enquiry.

'She does have feelings too, you know. I'm worried about her. I got a text from her last night asking me to ring her, so I did. She told me that she didn't tell the police everything. Apparently Miriam had talked about running away with her boyfriend. I told her she should tell the police if she's that worried but she won't.' She looked me in the eye. 'But then you know that don't you? Then she tells me the boyfriend's name is Khaled, she described what he looked like – I know it's him,' she it down on her lip. 'I want to have it out with him, but he's not answering his phone.'

'It's probably best to leave it for a bit – anyway, we don't know for sure it's him. Why don't you try and find out – I can help you – if you want? I feel kind of involved now.'

She sniffed and narrowed her eyes.

'Weirdo. I thought you were strange at primary school and you haven't changed.' She thought for a

73

moment. 'Helen's coming over here tomorrow. Do you want to meet up?'

Yes! Mentally I punched the air. 'OK,' I said, 'Thanks.'

'Don't get me wrong, I still don't get what you're up to, but I need to understand about Khaled. And don't harass her, OK?'

'Whatever.' I wasn't planning on taking orders from Fiona. I could hear voices in the shop. I stood up. 'I'll be there tomorrow, OK. Text me. Tess has got my number.'

She nodded, and I went back into the shop to relieve Gladys. Fiona looked back when she reached the door and stared at me, before disappearing out into the street.

CHAPTER 14

I walked through the front door and stopped. Mum was pacing round the living room, shouting into her mobile. As soon as I walked in she cut the other person off and threw her phone onto the sofa. It bounced onto the floor with a worrying clatter. Mum gets through a lot of phones.

'Who was that?' I asked, my stomach churning. She sank down onto the sofa, clutching her head in her hands. 'Mum?' I said.

'It was your father,' she replied. 'I knew this was a bad idea.'

'What's happened?' I asked. 'I thought you were OK with it now. The tickets have come and everything. Don't tell me you're going to change your mind.'

'No of course not, but I stupidly thought I wouldn't have to deal with your father. He rang me to talk over your plans and caught me off guard. I've already told him to contact me by email but does he ever listen? I'd forgotten how irritating he is.'

'Great. It's me that is going to stay with him, not you.'

'He won't irritate you; he just rubs me up the wrong way. He always has done and I should have listened to my mother when she warned me not to marry him. See,' she waved her finger at me, 'you should always listen to your mother.'

I rolled my eyes. 'So what does he want to tell you? I thought we'd arranged it all – He's meeting me at the Gare du Nord when my train gets in. I'd better carry one of those boards with my name on – he won't have a clue who I am.'

'Jas,' said Mum, shaking her head. 'Of course he'll recognise you, he's your father.' I snorted. 'Besides, he's seen you on Skype. I don't know what else he wanted – he said he needed to tell me something but I didn't give him a chance to speak. I've already told him he needs to speak to you directly.' She sighed. 'I suppose I was a bit hasty. Oh well, I'm sure it wasn't important.'

'Are we still going shopping on Friday?' She looked at me blankly for a moment. 'For France? I need some things, remember?'

'Oh yes, of course.' I knew she'd forgotten. 'I'm going over to Mark's tonight to watch his band practice,' I called over my shoulder as I ran upstairs.

Sadie was on my mind again. Why did she have to know Khaled? It complicated things. I doubted she was involved with him – she already had two boyfriends on the go as it was. I slapped my forehead. Maybe he was the Mystery Man! I logged onto her Facebook page. Neither Khaled nor Fiona were listed as friends. Just to be sure I typed in the name Miriam Jackson but nothing came up. Tess was friends with Khaled so I clicked via her page onto his, but his listing was private. I went back to Sadie's page. She had added a whole load of photos from a party at the weekend – her and her boyfriend AJ looking totally loved up. I looked at each shot closely but didn't recognise any of the background characters; in particular I was looking for Mystery Man/Khaled. Nothing. I only had two days left before I went to France and too many things to do in that short time. I made a list prioritising my time.

See Khaled
Speak to Fiona and Helen
Shop for clothes
Visit Gran with Mum?

I hesitated before adding the last point. Mum said I had to visit Gran before I went but I was hoping to try and get out of it. I hadn't recovered from last time. Mum planned to take me after we'd been shopping. I had phoned Tess and told her about Fiona's visit and she'd invited me over that evening.

'Mark's band are rehearsing, but he won't mind.'

'Khaled won't want to see me,' I argued. 'He'll associate me with Fiona.'

'Why? He knows you don't hang around with her – she wasn't particularly friendly, was she? We can go down and listen to the music. You won't be able to escape the music when you come to stay. They're not that good though, be warned.'

At six o clock that evening I was standing outside Mark's flat, waiting for Tes to answer the front door. I could hear a deep beat thumping out from the basement downstairs; the band must be here already. I'd seen them once at a school fundraising event, but that was a while ago and they'd been doing some serious practise since then.

Tess led me down a steep set of uncarpeted steps and I hung onto the railing as I went down. The guys were rehearsing in a long oblong space. The music wasn't bad, a rock beat provided by Des on drums, Khaled on bass and Mark playing guitar and singing. Mark's voice was deep and soulful and Tess and I sat together on the floor, backs against the wall and listened to the set. Mark was wearing a white t-shirt and jeans, his skinny hips writhing around to the beat. He was wearing a pork pie hat, which on anyone else would look ridiculous. Tess nudged me.

'Stop staring,' she said. I blushed, glad the room wasn't very well lit – not a lot of light got in down here and the lamp was dull and yellow. Mark was kind of nice looking.

'Des,' shouted Mark suddenly, making us jump and look up. 'You've played it wrong again – I keep telling you.'

'OK guys,' Khaled intervened putting his guitar down on the floor, 'time for a break, I think.' He went over to a rucksack which was placed by the door and the ensuing clinking sound was music to my ears as he pulled out a six pack of beer bottles and a couple of cans of coke. He handed a bottle each to Mark and Des. 'I didn't realise we'd have company,' he said, looking straight at me. 'Beer?' he held a bottle out to me.

'Thanks,' I said, aware of all eyes on me.

'Tess?' he turned to her.

'No way,' she said, pulling a face. 'Beer is gross and undignified. I'm surprised at you Jas.' I avoided her

78

eyes. He passed her a coke and flicked one open for himself, sitting down near us on the floor.

I shrugged, sipping at the cool lager. It slid down easily and I allowed myself to relax.

'Thirsty?' Mark asked and directed a smile straight at me. I took another gulp of beer, hoping to cool the heat of my face. He put down his guitar and came and joined the three of us on the floor. Des stayed tapping softly on his drums, going over and over the rhythm. I had never spoken to Des – he was very quiet and geeky – totally obsessed with music according to Tess. He works in the music shop in town, which is where Mark had met him.

'I heard about you and Fiona,' said Tess to Khaled. He punched his leg.

'You girls, man, do you have to talk about everything?'

'What's that?' asked Mark.

'They've split up,' Tess said. 'Khaled and Fiona.'

Khaled was shaking his head. 'You are so annoying Tess. I can't keep nothing secret around here.'

'Sorry to hear that mate.'

Khaled shrugged. 'Plenty more fish in the sea and all that.'

'Are you going out with Sadie now?' That was Tess. I couldn't believe her sometimes. Khaled exploded. 'Don't you start! I hardly know the chick.' He looked uncomfortable.

'Sadie? Posh Sadie?' Mark grinned. 'You're a dark horse mate.'

The background drumming had stopped. Des was listening in too.

79

'Yeah her. I know her, so what? And I spoke to her
– is that a crime?' He looked at me. 'I'm glad to see the
back of Fiona, she was way too possessive. Always
wanting to know where I was. You know that weekend
we went to the gig?' he looked at Mark. Mark nodded.
'She gave me hell after that, said she'd been trying to
ring me and why didn't I answer, where had I been? I'd
told her we were going to a concert and I wouldn't be
able to hear my phone. She wouldn't let it rest. She
wasn't even home that weekend – she was on that
course so I don't get why she was so bothered what I
was doing.'

'What was the concert?' I asked.

The Flying Toucans. They played the Roundhouse. It
was fantastic.'

Mark nodded agreement. 'We crashed over at my
mate Toby's and we went round Camden Market the
next day to pick up some new gear for the band. It was
a great weekend. Shame you missed it, Des.'

'Some of us have work to go to mate.' Des grinned
and started tapping at his drums again, the rhythm
familiar already. The music sounded OK to me; Tess
just didn't want to admit that her brother had talent.

'Time to get back to work,' said Mark and they both
got to their feet. 'Let's try out our new number on our
groupies.' He grinned at me and I couldn't help
grinning back. I swilled the remains of my beer. 'Help
yourself to another,' Khaled called out.

'Don't mind if I do,' I smiled, relaxed now and
settled back to watch the rehearsal. I had a funny
feeling I knew exactly which weekend the *Flying Toucans*
had been playing in London. I love it when the jigsaw

pieces that had been muddled up in a huge pile started slowly falling into place. My jigsaw still had plenty of gaps, but I was making good progress.

CHAPTER 15

'Yes!' I threw my fist up and jumped around my bedroom floor. I was right. *The Flying Toucans* had played The Roundhouse the weekend of May 26th – the weekend Miriam had been found. I made a tick against my checklist. Khaled and Mark had stayed over with a mate of Mark's that night. I needed to find out whether Mark had been with Khaled the whole time. As Miriam's boyfriend he was now high on my list of suspects. Tess could find out easily enough.

My phone flashed at me. A text from Fiona:

Meet tomorrow at 11 by the swings in Carisbrooke Park

I took off my headphones and went downstairs. Mum was passed out on the sofa, wine glass at her side. The television was on low. I watched her chest going up and down, a sheet of paper quivering in her hands. I removed the paper.

'Mum,' I called. No response. 'Mum.' That was loud. She opened her eyes then manoeuvred herself into a sitting position.

'Jas. I must have dropped off. Are you alright?'

'I'm going to the park in the morning with some friends.'

'That's great. I'm so glad you're getting out more, but don't forget your studies.'

'School has finished Mum. Give me a break.'

'Oh yes,' she said, 'I forgot.' Her eyes were starting to droop. I picked up the remote and turned the television off.

'I'm going to bed and I think you should too.'

A snore spluttered from her mouth; I was wasting my time. I dimmed the lamp and went off upstairs.

The park was busy next morning. Some sort of extreme workout class was taking place and I watched as a man wearing khaki uniform barked orders at a group of middle-aged women who looked like they would be more comfortable in a cake shop. As they lumbered back and forwards between trees I swung my legs until I had a steady rhythm going with the swing. I spotted Fiona and Helen making their way towards me. As they got closer and grew to their proper height, I could see that they were deep in conversation. I waved and Helen waved back.

'Hey,' I said.

Fiona nodded at me and Helen smiled shyly.

'Shall we go over to the shelter?' suggested Fiona. 'It's a bit windy out here and I spent ages on my hair this morning.' Her hair was sleek and straight. I had stuck a beanie on my head and barely noticed the wind.

'OK,' I said and jumped off the swing, stumbling. Helen caught my arm. 'Thanks,' I said. 'How long are you here for?'

'Just today – Auntie Lou is picking me up from Fiona's at six.'

The shelter was a grey concrete building covered in graffiti – big strokes of brightly coloured paint dragged into letters. Teenagers hung out here all the time, puffing on furtive cigarettes and snogging in the corner. Today it was empty and the sun shone into the shelter, making it look quite cosy. Fiona and I sat down on the bench, and Helen threw her padded jacket onto the ground and sat on it, cross-legged. She looked much younger than her years; the plaits didn't help, plus she chewed her nails constantly. Fiona lit a cigarette and blew the smoke in my direction.

'Tell Helen what you told me,' she said.

'It's nothing,' I laughed nervously. 'I like finding things out, I always have.' I shrugged. 'I'm good at it. When I read about the girl being killed in the paper, I wanted to know what had happened to her – I can relate to it, it's kind of scary – do you know what I mean? Then when I saw your name in the paper and I realised you might be a friend of Tess, I got a bit excited. Sad, I know, but I dragged Tess down to Keston and we found Helen.' Helen's eyes were fixed on me. 'I'm sorry I lied but your aunt caught me by surprise. All we were going to do was look at the house and check out the area. Just to get a feel of the place. That's what they do in books.' Disbelief was stamped all over Fiona's face. I hurried on. 'I know it's a bit eccentric. Then before I knew it we were actually talking to you and there was no way out of it...then when you mentioned Khaled... '

'What?' said Fiona.

'Well obviously Tess and I put two and two together and decided that Miriam was going out with the same

84

Khaled as you. Stupid really, but it's not a common name round here, is it?' Helen was staring at me wide-eyed, biting her fingernails furiously.

'Stop biting your nails,' I barked. She looked shocked and put her hands under her legs, squashing them out of sight with her thighs. I sighed. 'Sorry,' I said, 'it's just that I was...'

'Get on with the story,' said Fiona. Our eyes locked for a moment. I looked away first.

'Well it did seem like a big coincidence,' I said, 'And Tess thought the same. Then I found out that Khaled was away that weekend and you thought he was seeing someone else... they went to The Roundhouse you know, I checked. But did he spend all night with Mark, or did he go elsewhere? That's what I need to find out.'

Fiona was avoiding eye contact. I opened my bag and took out my purse, extracting a printout of a sheet of photos. Fiona caught sight of it and grabbed it out of my hands. 'Where did you get this?'

'Online. I thought Helen could look at it and tell us for sure if it's the same person. I wasn't going to tell you about Khaled and Miriam, Fiona, no way, it was none of my business; I just wanted to find out what was going on. Tess was pretty cut up about it. But then you split up with him anyway...' Fiona handed the sheet to Helen. She barely cast her eye over it before nodding.

'That's him. That's Miriam's boyfriend.'

Fiona dropped her head in her hands. Helen looked embarrassed; her fingernail had found its way into her mouth again. We sat in silence for a moment, then Fiona raised her head. She looked pale and defeated.

'I'm glad in a way,' she said. 'It's easier to hate him knowing that he's involved in something like this.'

'He's not necessarily involved,' I pointed out.

'You know what I mean.'

There was a movement to my right and I realised that Helen was crying. Big fat tears dropped over her cheeks.

'It's all my fault,' she said, 'I should have kept quiet.'

'Come here,' said Fiona and put her arm around Helen, pulling her towards her. They clung together, with me on the outside, looking in. 'You did the right thing.' She looked up at me and I nodded agreement.

We were all lost in thought for a moment. Finally Fiona picked up the sheet of photographs, scrunched it into a ball and threw it as far as she could. 'He was a rubbish boyfriend anyway.' Helen giggled, wiping her eyes with the back of her hand. 'But I'm going to find out what he was up to that weekend.' She looked at me, her blues eyes piercing mine. 'And you are going to help me, Miss Detective.'

'And me,' said Helen, 'You can't leave me out.' She pulled a pink notepad out of her bag along with matching pen and wrote the word CLUES in large square letters at the top of the page. She stuck her tongue out with concentration as she wrote. Then she wrote SUSPECTS on the opposite page. Fiona looked at me and we both burst out laughing.

CHAPTER 16

I kicked the wall, then looked back at the mirror. The shoes were wrong and the shirt didn't fit properly. I turned to the side. That was even worse. This was what happened when I tried to find a look for myself. Nothing matched. Maybe I was colour blind. My hair was sleek and shining, but what good was that to me now? I sighed. She'd done me a favour really. Everything was going to have to change.

I'd been round to Sadie's yesterday after I'd left Fiona and Helen, having convinced myself that Khaled was the Mystery Man. I sat on the bench conveniently placed opposite Sadie's house and pulled my beanie down over my head. There was no sign of the man with the bike this time; there was hardly any traffic at all. I was half reading a free paper which I'd picked up at the station. Miriam was still in the news but the story was further to the back of the paper now. The information was the same old stuff regurgitated. A door slammed and I looked up. A girl was coming out of Sadie's house. As she walked down the drive and turned into the street my heart picked up pace. I knew that walk, but...

I narrowed my eyes. The girl definitely moved in a familiar manner. She tossed her head and shook her chestnut coloured long hair. It was gorgeous. It was

Sadie! She must have had extensions put in. That cost a fortune! She was disappearing down the road so I left the newspaper on the bench and set off after her. It had taken me so long to achieve the perfect likeness and now she had ruined it all. She'd made me feel stupid. I walked faster, trying to breathe deeply.

I wasn't far behind Sadie now, so I slowed my pace. She'd taken her phone out of her bag and was talking into the receiver. She looked around as she talked, as if someone was telling her where something was. Then she waved and put the phone back into her pocket. A car I recognised was coming down the road. I quickly knelt down, pretending to tie my shoelace, keeping one eye on the car. It was Mystery Man. This time she got straight into the passenger side, a grim look on her face. What was she playing at?

The car had sped off and I had gone straight home and poured out a small glass of Mum's wine. I was getting used to the taste and I liked the way it made my head go fizzy. Back in my bedroom, I had put the glass down and stared at the mirror. I watched as my reflection ripped the shirt over my head and threw it onto the floor. My clothes were wrong because the hair was wrong. My head was all muddled. I kicked the shoes off and went into the bathroom, extracting a pair of scissors from the bathroom cupboard. I hesitated for a second, then took the scissors to my hair, hacking it off as quickly as I could. Large red clumps fell to the floor, spilling around me like drops of blood. I stared at my face the whole time, anger propelling the scissors as they chopped more and more chunks until my hair stood in tufts on my head. I threw the scissors into the sink and went back into my bedroom. I felt better now, strangely relieved of a burden. I blanked what I had done from my mind and sat down on the floor, pulling my laptop down onto my lap. Mentally I added finding out whether Khaled could drive or not to my to-do list. I clicked open my emails where I was surprised to find one from Michael.

Hi Jasmine, It's not long now until your visit and I can't wait to see you. We are looking forward to visiting Paris with you - it's a beautiful city — and then hopefully you will come and visit our home in Amersham. I'm attaching a recent photograph so you know who to expect when you arrive at the Gare du Nord. Love, Michael.

Curious, I clicked on the photo and a familiar face filled the screen. It was taken outside an old building. A man and a woman smiling broadly for the camera. Tears welled up inside me. He looked so familiar. I knew the woman too, I should have realised; she was the woman in the passport photo. They were both smiling, they looked happy. I stared at Michael's face; wishing answers would jump out of the photograph. Why had he abandoned us? A rage started bubbling up inside me and I snapped the laptop closed. At the same time my phone vibrated in my pocket. I pulled it out and looked at the handset. It was a text from an unknown number. I opened the message. It was from Mark, asking me if I wanted to meet up before I went away. Mixed emotions went through me. He was kind of alright, but I didn't have time to get involved with a boy. However, I needed to find out about that weekend away. I texted back:

Where and when?

His reply was instant:

Breakfast 9am Starbucks

I jumped up and went downstairs. I poured myself another drink and settled down in front of the television. Pictures flickered in front of me but in my mind all I could see was Sadie and her new hairstyle. I could change the colour but there was no way I could have extensions. Why couldn't I just be myself? The picture in my head changed, Michael and his glamorous new wife sprang into view. Except she wasn't a new wife at all, they'd been married for years.

'Jasmine, are you home?'

I drained my glass and padded out into the hall to greet Mum. My head felt a bit fuzzy. I went back and lay down on the sofa. Mum was pouring herself some wine in the kitchen.

'Are you OK?' she asked, filling the doorway and blocking out the light.

'Tired,' I said. 'I've got so much to do and I haven't even thought about packing.'

She came over to the sofa then did a double take when she caught sight of my hair. 'Jasmine! What the hell have you done? How could you?' She was shaking her head in disbelief.

I shrugged my shoulders, avoiding her eyes.

'I got sick of it. Anyway, I haven't got time to go to the hairdressers now have I? Don't forget we're going shopping tomorrow.'

Mum stared at me.

'You can't go anywhere looking like that. What on

90

earth will your father think?'

'Leave it Mum,' I said between clenched teeth. 'He has even less say than you do about the state of my hair. I like it OK?' I was lying, regretting my spontaneous action now, but there wasn't much I could do. She took a sip of her drink and sat down next to me.

'So have you remembered about tomorrow?' I repeated.

'Tomorrow?'

'Yes, Friday, the day before I go away, remember? The day you take me shopping and buy me loads of clothes?'

'Jasmine, please.' Mum hated me being sarcastic.

'Well you've forgotten haven't you? I can tell. Have you actually remembered that I am going away?' I looked at my phone. 'In approximately twenty eight hours' time I am going on my own to a strange country to stay with people that I don't know, while you go swanning off to America. The least you can do is take me shopping to cheer me up.'

Mum took a large gulp of her drink.

'I haven't forgotten, but something's come up. I'm sorry darling, but I can't possibly get tomorrow off. I need to be in the office. I'll give you some money; can't you take Tess out shopping with you?'

'I suppose so – if she's free.' I didn't want to go shopping with Mum in the least but I wished she hadn't so clearly forgotten me and made other plans.

'I'll make you something nice to eat tomorrow evening and help you pack to make it up to you. How's that? You can show me what you've bought. I'll take you to the station and see you off on Saturday, of course.'

'Don't go mad,' I said. At least she'd forgotten about seeing Gran. Mum went back to the kitchen and I reached over and took a large swig of her wine.

'Dad sent me a photo of his wife,' I said to Mum when she came back in with a plate of sandwiches for us. 'She's very pretty.'

'So I've heard,' said Mum, curling her lip.

'I bet she's stuck up.'

'Gran met her once.' She slapped her head against her forehead. 'I was meant to take you to see Gran as well. What is the matter with my brain these days?'

'I won't have time to see Gran. I'll see her when I get back.'

'OK,' she looked relieved.

'I'm going to bed now,' I announced, when I'd had enough to eat. The wine had made me feel very sleepy. 'I'm getting up early tomorrow. I'm meeting a friend for breakfast.'

Mum raised her eyebrows. 'I don't know what's come over you lately,' she said. 'You're getting very sociable all of a sudden.'

'No I'm not,' I said. 'Anyway since when did you ever notice what I get up to?'

Mum looked hurt. 'I notice everything you do,' she said, 'and I'm sorry I'm having to send you away, but this job in New York will hopefully secure me a lot more work over the next few months.'

She didn't get it, it wasn't about the money for me, more work would mean her spending even less time at home.

'Night,' I said, picking up my plate to put it into the dishwasher. Mum grabbed my hand as I went past.

'I am sorry about the shopping. I'll leave some money out in the kitchen OK, in case I go out before you. And maybe you could find time to get a quick hair cut?'

I pulled my hand away. 'Forget it Mum. It's my hair so get used to it. It'll have grown back by the time we see each other again.'

'I suppose you're right,' she said doubtfully.

'See you in the morning.' I cursed as I tripped over Mum's bag which she had plonked in the doorway, I glanced at her, my breath held in tightly. I needn't have worried. As usual she was oblivious to me, her eyes closed, head resting back on the sofa. Would she even notice when I wasn't there?

CHAPTER 17

A beeping noise was piercing my head. I pulled the pillow over my ears. It didn't go away. I realised it was my alarm. I stretched my arm out of bed, picked up my phone and turned it off. My head felt a bit thick. I had woken up in the night and been unable to sleep for ages, before falling into a nightmare about being lost in a foreign country, desperately trying to find the Eiffel Tower, but nobody could understand what I was saying.

It was eight thirty, half an hour to go before I had to meet Mark. I ran my hands over my head. The uneven tufts reminded me. The hair cut. *Why Jasmine?*

I had a quick shower and dressed in dark jeans and my favourite grey sweatshirt. I attempted to dry my hair into some sort of style, failing miserably. I pulled my beanie over it in disgust. I pulled on my red converse and grabbed my keys. Mum had left me some money on the table, which I dropped into my purse. At least she hadn't forgotten that.

Mark was already sitting in the café, a plate of sausages, bacon and beans in front of him. I ordered a tea and a chocolate croissant. He was wearing dark jeans and a t-shirt; I had rarely seen him wear anything else. The same hat he had been wearing last night covered his short dark hair.

'Are you practising for France?' he asked, nodding at

my chocolate croissant. 'Un pain au chocolat pour Mademoiselle.'

'Do you speak French?' I was impressed.

'Hardly. It's one of the few things I remember from school. 'A croque-monsieur is the other, but I couldn't tell you what it is.'

'I'll find out and let you know,' I said, biting into my pastry, brown flakes snowing down over my plate. 'Thanks for saying I can stay, by the way.'

'No worries. Are you looking forward to going to France?' he asked.

I pulled a face. 'Not really. Well, kind of. It's complicated.'

'I like complicated,' he said, grinning.

'Well I'm spending a few days with my dad and his wife in Paris, but remember, this is the dad who abandoned us when I was a baby and I haven't seen since.'

'You must have spoken to him at least, surely?'

'He's emailed me and we talked once on Skype. It was weird. Part of me wants to go, but most of me hates him for leaving us. I'm a bit scared, to be honest. I don't want to meet his wife, although I've seen a photo and she looks really nice. Plus I'd much rather be in New York – although not necessarily with Mum.'

Mark took a swig of tea. 'I thought Tess said you wanted to stay with us?'

I put my hands over my face. 'You must think I'm so rude,' I said. 'I really do want to stay with her – and you – I was only joking about New York . . .'

'Forget it,' he said, 'I'm only teasing.' He mopped up his plate with a piece of toast.

95

'So what did you think of the band?' he asked. I was grateful for the change of subject.

'Not bad,' I said. 'You've improved a lot since that gig at school.'

He laughed. 'Khaled's the reason,' he said. 'He makes us work really hard. He wants to make it big.'

'I'm surprised,' I said, 'he doesn't seem that serious about anything. He didn't seem bothered about splitting up with Fiona.'

Mark shook his head. 'I knew that was going to happen. He wasn't that committed to her.'

'Why do you say that?'

'I'm not sure I should talk about it really.' He scratched his head. 'Well, just don't say anything to Tess, OK?'

'No worries.'

'You know that weekend we went away together, to stay at my mates' flat in Camden?'

I nodded.

'Well I think he was seeing someone else. We went to the concert together but he left early and wouldn't tell me where he was going. I think he was worried I would tell Tess and Fiona would find out. He came back really late – in the early hours of the morning. His boots were covered in mud – I don't know what he'd been up to. He got annoyed when I started teasing him about it so I haven't mentioned it since. I'm glad Fiona knows the truth; she's better off out of it. I would never two-time someone. What's the point? I would only go out with someone if I really liked them, so why go off with someone else? Idiot.'

'I'm glad he's told Fiona too,' I said.

'I thought you two didn't get on?'

'We didn't get on at primary school, but…' I glanced at my watch.

'Do you have to go?' asked Mark.

I nodded. 'I've got to buy some stuff for France and I need to pack, and…'

'No worries.'

We hovered awkwardly outside the café. 'Which way are you going?' he asked.

'Into town. I need some hair dye.'

'What colour will it be this time?'

'Brown. I'm sick of this red.'

'It will suit you. To be honest, your hair looks too much like that Sadie's – you know the one who caused all the trouble with Khaled, although I think he just used that as an excuse to break up with Fiona. You don't want to look like her.'

Colour rushed into my cheeks. 'Why do you say that?'

'She's so fake. Her brother's thinking of joining our band so I've run into her a few times. She's a bit snooty. You've got lovely hair, it will look better brown.'

He wouldn't be saying that if he could see my effort at DIY hair styling.

'I think Sadie looks good.'

'She's not original, though, is she? She looks like a hundred other girls. I prefer people who stand out from the crowd.'

His words were running through my head as I set off towards the town centre. Nobody had ever called my hair lovely before. The chemist was fairly empty as

97

it was still early and I spent ages looking at the vast array of boxes of hair dye in front of me, each with a pretty girl and a plastic smile on the front. I settled for a chocolate brown colour, that should be dark enough to cover the red. Mark had got me thinking; I was going to be quite anonymous in France. It would be good to cultivate a new image for a couple of weeks, a sort of trial run.

I loaded up my basket with travel stuff for my journey, lots of cute miniature creams and gels.

'Going on holiday?' asked the sales assistant.

I nodded, although I wasn't sure exactly how much of a holiday it was going to be. I spent the rest of the morning buying clothes, mostly boring items such as tights and underwear, but I did buy a cool pair of turquoise jeans. They would look great with my new black boots. It struck me that this was the first thing I had bought for ages that wasn't recommended by *Sadiestyle*. It felt wrong somehow, but also liberating. Was it because of what Mark had said? I didn't think so. What did he know about fashion after all?

My phone rang as I left the store. I put my bag on a nearby bench and sat down to take the call. It was Tess.

'You're off tomorrow aren't you?' she asked. 'Do you want to meet up?'

I made my way over to the café in the precinct. The walls were lined with books and there was a stationery shop where you could browse as you waited for your food. I ordered a sandwich and an apple juice, then sat down to wait for Tess. I chose a seat next to the window and watched the people going in and out of shops, stopping to chat, light a cigarette or take a call. I saw Tess approaching but she wasn't on her own, Fiona was with her. I breathed deeply as I waved at them and seconds later they had joined me at the table.

Tess went off to join the queue and Fiona sat down. Her make up looked thicker than usual.

'I spoke to Mark,' I said. 'Khaled did go off that weekend, so he hasn't got an alibi for the whole night.'

'So it could have been him that went off to meet Miriam.' Fiona's eyes flashed. 'How can we find out?'

'I'm working on that,' I said. 'But you know I'm going to France tomorrow so we'll have to stay in touch online. Give me your email address and how to get in touch with you.'

'I'll text it to you,' she said and started pushing buttons on her phone. Tess came back to the table with two cans of diet coke, glasses and straws.

'So you two are friends now?' she asked, looking from me to Fiona.

She shrugged. 'We're helping Helen out, and Jasmine is seeing to a bit of unfinished business for me.'

My phone pinged as Fiona's message came through.

'Have you heard from Helen?' I asked.

Fiona rolled her eyes. 'Only about every other minute. She thinks we're the Famous Five. Except there's only three of us.'

'Four,' said Tess indignantly. 'I brought you all together remember? Besides, when Jas is in France I will be taking over the operation.'

'Operation! I thought Helen was bad enough,' said Fiona.

'Look, if you don't want to do this...' I glared.

'Calm down,' said Tess, 'let's just chill out, for God's sake.'

I took a mouthful of apple juice and finished off my sandwich.

'I forgot to tell you Fiona, I checked on Facebook and I don't think there is anything going on between Khaled and Sadie.'

Fiona looked like she had just bitten on a lemon.

'He said to us there was nothing going on, at the rehearsal, didn't he Jasmine?'

'Tess is right.' I agreed. I didn't mention what he'd said about Fiona being possessive.

'What he says doesn't mean anything. I want to know for sure,' said Fiona sulkily.

'OK,' I said. 'Tess, can you try and speak to Khaled and find out a bit more about that weekend ... and about Sadie,' I added hastily, aware of Fiona's eyes on me. 'You're in the best position to do that after all, he'll be round at your house to see Mark for rehearsals.'

'Looks like this enquiry wouldn't be going very far without me,' said Tess. 'I'll have a go, but I can't promise he'll tell me anything.'

'I can't help having to go to France,' I said. 'It's only for the weekend. I'm sure I'll have had enough of them by then.'

A waitress appeared at our table with two plates of sandwiches and the conversation died out for a bit as they started eating. I watched Fiona out of the corner of my eye; she pulled a slice of ham out of her sandwich and picked at it a bit before pushing the plate to one side.

'I'm not hungry,' she said. 'I'm going home. Mum

wants me back by three.' She pushed her chair back and stood up. 'I'll be waiting to hear from you, so don't forget, OK?' she said.

Tess and I watched her walk briskly across the square, her thin shoulders rigid, before she disappeared from view.

'Why did that sound like a threat? She still doesn't trust me.'

'She's still hurting about splitting up with Khaled,' Tess reminded me. 'Give her a break.'

Tess walked back to the bus stop with me. 'How long do you think you'll be gone for?'

'It depends on how we get on. It might be good if I go to Amersham, see where Michael lives, find out more about him. Try and Skype me without laughing, I can't help what I look like.'

'You're such an idiot, Jas!' she said, punching me. The bus arrived at that moment and I waved back at her until she had disappeared from view. I felt strangely empty.

I opened the front door and was greeted by the sight of a luxurious luggage set in the hallway.

'Mum,' I called out excitedly and she came out of the kitchen, wiping her hands on a tea towel. 'It's gorgeous!' I said. There was one medium size black leather case with a small holdall that fitted on top. The kind of luggage Sadie would have. Damn! Why did she keep popping up? 'I was going to take my old rucksack.'

'You can't travel with that,' Mum said. 'What would your father think?'

My face dropped. 'Is that what this is all about?'

'No,' she said indignantly. 'I wanted to make up for letting you down today and I managed to get off early. I've cooked us a mushroom risotto and some salad so we can have that later.' I gave her a hug and she looked surprised.

'I'll go and have a shower then do some packing. Can we eat after that?'

Mum nodded and I went off upstairs. The first thing I did was go into my bathroom and put the hair dye on. I left it on for thirty minutes to make sure the colour took. I wanted the red to be a thing of the past. I wrapped a plastic bag around my head and started sorting out what I wanted to pack. I was starting to feel edgy about meeting Michael.

Mum called upstairs that she was popping out to the shop so I took the opportunity to run downstairs and get myself a drink. An icy looking bottle of vodka lay on the top shelf. I poured the clear liquid into a glass and took a can of diet coke out of the fridge. It tasted much better than wine. I went back upstairs and washed the colour out of my hair. The smell made my eyes water, but the results were worth it. I stared into the mirror. I looked more like I used to, before Sadie, my hair a chocolate shade of brown. I dried my hair under the dryer then rubbed some hair clay in. It didn't look too bad. I put some music on, then set about packing my case.

Mum looked shocked when I went downstairs.

'What have you done to your hair now?' she asked. She stepped back and studied it. 'Actually, it doesn't look too bad. I never could get used to that red. It wasn't you somehow. It suits you short, but maybe try a hairdresser next time eh?'

After dinner I watched TV for a bit, then went upstairs to check my emails before I went to bed. I clicked onto Sadie's site, but seeing her new hairstyle in her profile picture put me in a bad mood. I turned the computer off and got ready for bed, exhausted after such a long day. Just as I was dropping off my phone buzzed. It was a text from Michael.

See you tomorrow at the Eurostar arrivals. I can't wait to see you. I have a surprise for you.

Great! Didn't he realise that meeting my father for the first time in my memory was going to be one hell of a surprise already? I sincerely hoped he didn't have anything else to spring on me. I turned my phone to silent and closed my eyes.

CHAPTER 18

I cursed my bag as it wedged itself in the way of the ticket barrier. I was thinking about Mum. She'd told me she had something important to tell me at the last minute as she waved me off at St Pancras, and left me wondering for the whole journey what it was she wanted to say. I scanned the people waiting behind the barriers, several men holding up pieces of cards with names on. Then I spotted Michael. I stopped walking, my legs suddenly feeling a bit wobbly. Even though the photograph that had been displayed in all the papers was burnt into my brain, it was still a shock to see him. But it wasn't just that that was making my heart clatter in my chest, it was the two policemen carrying machine guns standing behind him that prevented my feet from moving. Was I too late?

Then Michael raised his hand to wave and the policemen moved off. My stomach relaxed a little. I pushed my ticket into the gate and manoeuvred my bag through the barrier. Then he was at my side, taking my bag, his hand on my arm. I shook it off.

'Jasmine, how was your journey?'

'Fine,' I said.

He took a step backwards. 'Let me look at you. You've changed your hair colour.'

'I'm always changing my hair colour.' The dark clusters around his chin were new too. A disguise? 'You've got a beard.'

His face was a lot more creased than I expected. He had a tanned, weather beaten look about him.

'It suits you. Jasmine… come on, let's get a taxi.' I followed him out of the station, weaving through people, more heavily armed policemen. French conversation fluttered through the air all around me.

Outside the station was very noisy. The road was busy with traffic and people were seated outside a row of cafes on the opposite side of the road. Michael wheeled my bag around to the side away from the crowds and the next thing I knew I was being bundled into a taxi. Michael sat in the front and the driver struck up a conversation which involved a lot of waving of hands on the driver's part. My heart lurched every time he let go of the steering wheel, not helped by the craziness of the other cars on the road. Everything was moving very fast. I tried to take in the sights but couldn't concentrate. I studied the back of Michael's head. Every now and then he tried to catch my eye in the mirror. I stared resolutely out of the window. I recognised Notre Dame, and the metro signs, and we must have passed a hundred cafes, all identical looking. I saw a girl drinking a green liquid, which I recognised as being from the chapter on food and drink in our school textbook.

'Are you OK Jasmine?' Michael was asking. I nodded. 'It's not far now. We're staying at a hotel near the Bastille.'

We lurched through a few narrow streets, the driver impatiently honking on his horn. I had never experienced such noisy traffic before. Every now and then he slammed his hand down on the steering wheel and cursed loudly. I was glad I didn't know what he was saying.

We drove slowly along an energetic street full of small shops and cafes, then turned into a less busy narrow road, where the driver parked the car, leapt out and took my case out of the boot. Michael handed some notes to the driver and they shook hands. The street was made up of very tall old looking buildings. It was notably quiet after the hustle and bustle just around the corner.

'This is us,' said Michael, pointing to a large impersonal looking building, with hundreds of little windows looking down at us. 'Come on up. Sara can't wait to meet you. Caroline told you about Sara didn't she?'

Michael put his key in the tall wooden door and turned. He stepped inside.

I stayed outside the door.

'Sara? I thought her name was Nora?' A strange expression flittered across his face. 'I suppose you mean your wife. The one you abandoned us for.'

Concern erased the baffled expression from Michael's face.

'Jasmine,' he said. 'It wasn't really like that. There are things I need to tell you, but let's get you settled in first.' He took a step towards me, coming out of the doorway. 'You don't know how happy I am to see you.'

I shrugged and he turned away and I followed behind him and waited while he checked me in at the reception. He spoke fast fluent French and although I didn't want to be, I was impressed. Then we stepped into a tiny lift, where I was much closer to him than I was comfortable with. I held tightly onto my case until the lift had creaked it's way impossibly slowly to the fifth floor.

'Come and meet Sara, then I'll show you to your room. We're only a couple of doors along from you.'

I walked along in a sort of trance. I couldn't quite believe that I was really with my father, and he was behaving like it was all completely normal. I pulled my bag into the doorway, letting it prop the door half open.

The room was large, plain and very white, with a double bed, comfy chair, a flat screen television and not much else in it. A tall woman was standing by the window.

'Jasmine,' she said, 'I'm so pleased to meet you.' She was incredibly pretty, with shoulder length dark hair. She was wearing a neat skirt suit and a scarf around her neck. Her eyes and skin were dark brown. She spoke English with a heavy French accent. 'Please come and sit down.'

I sat down on the chair. It was soft and squishy and I sank down into it, suddenly exhausted.

'Can I get you a drink?' she asked.

'Just water please,' I said. She opened a tiny fridge which was hidden under the TV, poured out a glass and set it down at my side. I looked around.

Michael hovered by the side of the bed. 'I know this

is a very strange situation,' he looked at Sara — 'for all of us. I'm going to show you to your room and let you relax for a bit, then we'll all have something to eat and try and get to know one another. I want you to feel at home here.'

'Michael,' Sara said. 'When are you going to tell Jasmine...?'

Michael cast a warning look at Sara and surprise registered on her face. He shook his head.

'We'll talk later,' he said, raising his voice. She looked uncomfortable.

'Do you need to let Caroline know you are here?' he asked me. 'You can use the telephone in your room.'

'It's OK, I'll text her later.' I said. 'I'm a bit tired.'

'Let me show you to your room,' said Sara. 'I'll help you with your bag.'

She took my case, which was leaning against the wall and frowned at the weight of it. 'It's heavy!' she exclaimed.

'I'll do it,' I said, taking the handle from her. At that moment there was a knock at the door. Sara pushed past Michael, opened the door and spoke rapidly in French. I couldn't see who she was speaking to. She sounded agitated. She came back into the room followed by a young girl.

'But Maman,' the girl was saying as she came in, stopping mid-sentence when she caught sight of me. She looked about my age; she was slim, wearing a dark jacket and jeans. A white headscarf was draped around her head. She had the same dark skin as Sara. She stared at me and her mouth fell open in surprise. I stared back, feeling suddenly dizzy. Who was this girl?

There was something familiar about her. We stared at each other. Michael came back into the room.

'What are you doing here?' His raised voice made me jump.

'Did you really expect me to stay away?' she said. Michael looked embarrassed.

'Are you going to tell me what's going on?' I asked. I couldn't take my eyes off the girl. She smiled at me.

'Hello Jasmine,' she said. 'I'm Malika. I'm your half-sister.'

CHAPTER 19

Something exploded inside my head. I pushed past the girl and ran out of the door, along the corridor, down all the stairs and out into the street. I hurtled blindly past a few doorways until I collided with a man. He shouted incomprehensible words at me and I ran again, turning into an alleyway, where I tried to control my breathing. My chest hurt. I took in several deep breaths until I could stand up straight. A shuffling noise behind me made me turn quickly, my heartbeat picking up pace.

Malika. My sister.

'Please,' she said. 'Don't run away again. I'm your friend.'

Looking at her up close gave me an extraordinary sensation. Her eyes were dark brown, and shaped just like Michael's. Gran always said I had Michael's eyes. Wisps of dark hair stuck out from under her scarf.

'Come with me,' she said, 'there's a little park around the corner, we can stay there for a moment.'

I followed her, not knowing what else to do, somehow drawn to her. She led me back out onto the main street, where we crossed the road and went into a small park opposite. It was tiny, but the bench we sat on was in the sun and was opposite an ice cream kiosk.

'Wait there,' she said, then disappeared off to the kiosk, coming back with two bottles of cold water.

I held the refreshingly cold bottle against my burning cheek, before taking a welcome sip.

'You didn't know about me, did you?'

I shook my head, my eyes filling with tears. Rage was making my head pound.

'I should never have come,' I said.

'Don't say that.' She turned around on the bench to face me, pulling her legs up under her. 'If you hadn't come we would never have met. You're my sister. I've always wanted a sister.'

Her eyes roamed over my face, looking into my eyes, as if searching for answers.

'How old are you?' I asked.

'Fourteen.'

I bit down on my lip until it hurt.

'And you?' she asked.

'Fifteen.'

I could see she was doing the same calculations in her head as I was doing in mine.

'How long have you known about me?' I asked.

'For about six months. But now everything makes sense. Papa has been strange for the last few weeks, acting as if something was about to happen. Yesterday he told me that you were coming here.'

Hearing her say 'Papa,' like that cut into me.

'Aren't you angry?' I asked.

'There are too many things in this world to be angry about. I wish he had told me earlier but I can't change the past. I'm just so glad you are here.'

'Why has he kept me a secret? I don't understand.' I stood up and started pacing up and down, the anger returning. 'Why did he tell you and not me?' A thought

111

suddenly occurred to me. I sat back down again, deflated. 'Does my mum know about this?' I shivered. Despite the sunshine a breeze had sprung up. Malika tucked a strand of hair back under her headscarf.

'Why are you wearing a headscarf?'

'I'm a Muslim,' she said.

'But your mum isn't wearing one.'

She shrugged. 'It's my choice.'

I put my head in my hands.

'This is mad. What am I doing here?' The sun had gone behind a cloud now. I pulled my jacket tighter around myself.

'You're shivering,' Malika said. 'Let's go back to the hotel.'

'When did you get here?'

'Only this morning. We've been staying with mum's friends in Lille for the past month. This is only my second visit to Paris.' She smiled at me. I hesitated, then smiled back.

'Come on,' she said, getting up off the bench.

'Wait,' I said.

'What is it?'

I closed my eyes, then opened them slowly.

'This isn't a dream,' I said. 'I wouldn't believe it only...you look like Michael. It must be true. I really do have a sister.'

She laughed. 'Of course it isn't a dream. If it is I don't ever want to wake up.' She held out her hand. I stared at it for a moment, then allowed her to enclose her fingers around mine and pull me up.

CHAPTER 20

My room had a view over the rooftops of Paris, lots of different shapes. A large gold coloured statue standing up high dominated the skyline. I lay down on the bed, shattered. The window was slightly open and the occasional voice drifted up from the street below. I couldn't be bothered to unpack. Malika's room was next door, and Michael and Sara's the other side. There was a knock at the door. I dragged my heavy limbs over to the door and opened it. Malika followed me back in.

'Do you want to come downstairs? There's a café – you must be hungry. Maman and Papa are down there.'

My appetite had disappeared the moment I first set eyes on Michael.

'OK,' I said. 'Let me just do something with my hair.' I took out my hair brush and attempted to drag some sort of style to my uneven locks. 'What's your hair like?'

She unfastened her scarf. Her hair tumbled past her shoulders, thick black and wavy.

'It's lovely,' I said.

'It's boring,' she said. 'Yours is . . . unusual, different.'

'Stop being polite. I took out my bad mood on it yesterday. It was red, but I changed it back to brown.'

Yesterday! That seemed like a lifetime away.

'What is it like where you live? Do you have a stepdad?'

'Don't you know anything about me?' She shook her head, refastening her scarf back around her head. It suited her. I wished I had a scarf to cover mine up with.

'There's just me and Mum, we live in London. Michael left her when I was a baby. She doesn't have anything to do with him. She's working in New York for a few days.'

'It's really strange,' she said, 'that your mother would allow you to come, don't you think? Did she mind?'

'It was my decision. I've always hated him too, for leaving us, but when he said he wanted to see me – I've always been intrigued, wondering what he was like, why he left, and ...' I bit down on my lip. I couldn't tell her my real reason for wanting to see him . . . 'well he is my dad.'

'Did he get in touch with your Mum, or was it the other way around?'

'Michael got in touch with Mum because he needed some papers. He came down to London to see her. I know that for a fact, it was in May.'

'I wonder if Maman knew.' She looked thoughtful for a moment, then jumped to her feet. 'Shall we go downstairs?' We waited outside the lift. I watched her, fascinated. She turned to me.

'I'm glad you know, that you came. I want to know everything about you.' I wished she wasn't being so nice. I didn't want to like her but it was hard not to.

I checked my phone on the way down in the lift, but

there was only one message from Mum asking me if I'd arrived safely. I sent a quick reply. Sara and Michael were seated in the café, talking. Sara stood up as we approached.

'Jasmine, how are you feeling? Would you like something to eat?' I shook my head. 'Just a coke please.'

Malika asked for a sandwich and Sara placed the orders.

'I am so sorry,' she said, 'it must have been a terrible shock for you, to find out that you have a sister like that.' She glared at Michael and I realised she was annoyed with him too. He poured himself a glass of water, then came over when he saw me looking at him.

'Jasmine,' he said. 'I'm so sorry – for everything – maybe one day you'll be able to forgive me.'

A waiter arrived with three large baguette type sandwiches on a tray.

'Mine's cheese,' said Malika, 'we can share if you want.'

My stomach had started growling at the sight of the food. I was hungry after all. Malika pushed the sandwich towards me and I took a bite of it, the soft brie melting in my mouth. Sara began to outline the ideas she had for places for us to visit. As she talked I took the opportunity to watch Michael. The beard made him look older. Had he grown it to make himself look different? He looked jumpy, uncomfortable.

As I watched him it was hard to keep images of Miriam Jackson from flashing into my mind. Why hadn't he stayed to report the crime?

My phone buzzed. Mum. She was off to America

the next day. As I started to reply my fingers froze mid-air – did Mum know about Malika? I stared down at the screen, anxious for none of them to see how I was suddenly feeling. Mum's face as she waved me off at the Eurostar terminal filled my mind, she was trying to tell me something important … surely she couldn't have known?

'Does Mum know about Malika?' The words blurted out of my mouth. I watched Michael's face. He glanced at Sara, then nodded. I tried to breathe, but the air caught in my throat.

'Jasmine, of course she knew.'

'What do you mean, *of course*?' I spat the last two words at him. All the hatred I'd ever felt for him came rushing to the surface.

'Jasmine,' Sara said, reaching out to touch my arm. I shook it off.

'I'm tired,' I said. I stood up and left the room.

Mum rang later that evening.

'Hey Jas,' she said. 'How was the journey?'

'Why didn't you tell me?'

'Tell you what, dear? Jasmine what are you talking about?'

'About my half-sister of course! It's just been the tiniest shock! How long have you known?'

She sighed. 'I've always known. Your father was away working in France and he met Sara on one of those trips. I knew straight away there was something going on; he told me he'd end it but then he found out she was pregnant. I threw him out. You were only tiny. How could he?' I heard the familiar sound of a bottle being opened, liquid sliding into a glass.

'Why didn't you tell me before?'

A long silence filled the miles between us.

'I had a breakdown after he'd left. I was still in love with him and I was devastated. Your Gran – his own mother – was so disgusted with him she moved in with me to help look after you. I shut out all knowledge of Michael and his new family, it was the only way I could cope. I know I should have told you, especially when I knew you were going to meet him, but, well, I ran out of time.' Her voice trailed off. She took a large swallow.

'By the way,' she said, 'a boy called round this afternoon.'

'A boy? Who?'

'He said his name was... hang on I've written it down somewhere...' I heard her put the phone down then a crash as something dropped to the floor and Mum cursing in the background.

'Mum?'

'I'm here,' she said, her words slightly slurred. 'Khaled,' she said, 'Khaled, that's who he was. He's very handsome Jasmine, you've been keeping him quiet haven't you?'

'For goodness' sake, Mum,' I said. 'He's in Mark's band.'

'There's no need to be like that. Oh look at the time, I'll have to go now darling, Carol wants me to call her before I go. Goodnight darling, sleep well. I'll ring you tomorrow.'

I was awoken by a whooshing noise from outside in the

street. I had no idea where I was. I propped myself up in bed and looked around the unfamiliar room. Everything was white. I was in France. I lay back down again, memories flooding in. Someone tapped lightly on the door. I opened it to reveal Malika carrying two cups in her hand.

'Room service,' she said. I couldn't help smiling, I had a sister. She sat down on the end of the bed and handed me a paper cup.

'There's a McDonalds on the corner.' she said.

I propped myself up and drank some coffee. It tasted good.

'What would you like to do today? Maman says I can show you around, be a tourist. Would you like that?'

'Just the two of us?' I asked.

She nodded. 'Papa wants you to have some time to yourself, think about things a bit. But if you want to be on your own...'

'No,' I said.

'He says you have friends in Paris, on the Champs-Elysées, do you want to meet up with them?'

I shook my head, embarrassed. I'd forgotten that I had said that.

'Another day, maybe.'

'It's very smart around there you know,' said Malika, 'who are they?'

'Forget it,' I said sharply. A shadow crossed her eyes and I hated myself.

'I'd rather get to know you,' I said. 'Where are we going today?'

Malika didn't know Paris well, but she knew a lot

about it. We spent the whole day getting on and off the tourist bus, tramping around looking at buildings. I saw the Eiffel Tower, Notre Dame and the Louvre, which I recognised from the cover of my school text book. After a couple of hours I was hungry and fed up with walking. Malika suggested we take some food down to the river. We pooled our money and bought two ham and cheese baguettes and two cans of coke, then went down a steep staircase to the side of the river Seine. The river was busy, there was a constant stream of tourist boats going by.

'I like walking,' she said. 'I walk around a lot, sit outside in cafes and watch people. Paris is great for that.' She opened her bag and pulled out a sketchpad. 'This is what I like to do,' she said shyly, 'would you like to see?'

She passed me the sketchpad which was full of sketches of buildings, people, and street scenes.

'You did these?' I asked. 'They're brilliant. Look at that, it's where we are now.' I pointed to a drawing of the river, the old majestic buildings on the opposite bank. She nodded. 'I did that last time I was here.' She took the book and flicked through to a drawing of a man and handed it to me. It was Michael. I gasped. The likeness was amazing. I closed the book quickly.

'It's difficult for you, coming here, isn't it?' she asked, 'seeing Michael again, finding out about me.'

'We could have been a normal family,' I said, fixing my eyes on a passing boat, people waving, getting smaller and smaller as they disappeared from sight. 'Mum, Dad and me. I used to moan about not having a brother or sister but I had my friends to play with. It

119

was Mum that was difficult to deal with. He ruined her dream of a family life; simple as that. It was easier for her to banish him from her memory. Mum wanted me to forget that I had a Dad and I wanted to remember him. Mum never got over him leaving. Everything is his fault. She works too much, she drinks too much, she's never at home. And then Gran got ill.' I swallowed hard, flinching at the memory. 'So now it's just me and Mum rattling around together. Then out of the blue she tells me Michael has been in touch! Can you imagine?' I stood up and started pacing up and down, agitated. 'And now I arrive here and discover that he has another daughter, barely younger than me.' My voice was getting louder but I couldn't stop myself. 'He was seeing your mum when he was with us… no wonder Mum hates him.'

I sat back down on the bench and put my head in my hands. Malika put her arm around me. I shook it off.

'Jasmine,' she said. 'Papa is a coward. I think he kept away for your mum's sake – he knew it was too painful for her. I always suspected he was hiding something.'

'What makes you say that?'

'He always refused to speak about the time before he met Maman. I knew he had been married before, that's all. I don't know anything about his parents, where he came from in England, it's all so strange. I have so many unanswered questions. That's why my identity is so important to me. I need to know who I am, it's all I have.'

'I get that,' I said, thinking of Sadie for the first time in ages. 'Sometimes I have no idea who I am.'

120

She put her hand on my arm and this time I let it rest there. 'We need each other,' she said. 'I'm starting to realise that Papa creates his own problems wherever he goes, so try not to take it personally.'

A passenger boat went by, a line of children waving from the top deck. Malika waved back.

We spent the afternoon at the Pompidou Centre, the strangest yet most interesting building I had ever seen. Afterwards we sat outside, watching a street busker entertaining the crowd. Malika got her sketch pad out, stroking her pencil across the page, bringing the crowd to life. Today she was wearing a red headscarf. A couple of people stood behind her, watching her draw. I was proud of her. She chewed on her lip, concentrating hard, as she recreated the scene in front of her, oblivious to the people observing her.

By the end of the afternoon I had come to a decision. I was going to tell Malika everything about Michael and his appearance on Crimewatch and what I had uncovered so far. There were too many questions going round in my head and I had a feeling my sister would be able to help me fill in the answers.

CHAPTER 21

Back at the hotel later that afternoon I had some time to myself before dinner. I went down to the hotel café and logged onto the internet. First I checked my emails. There were two, one from Fiona and one from Tess. I opened Fiona's first:

Hi Jasmine,
Have you found out anything about Khaled yet? I texted him and told him I knew he was going out with Miriam.
Fiona

What had she gone and done that for? I noticed she hadn't asked me about my trip. I was kidding myself that we were ever going to be friends. Tess had a lot more to say in her email:

Hi Jas,
How was the journey? France? Your old man? Is he still alive after meeting you? There have been a few developments here. Khaled came over for a rehearsal and I talked to him after and told him I knew that he had been going out with Miriam. OMG!! I know, yes I really did say that. I didn't tell him how I knew and I could tell he wasn't very happy cos he went all sulky after that. He said I'd better not tell. Also he said he hadn't spoken to the police because they didn't know he was her boyfriend. Can you believe that? Helen still hasn't told them – I

suppose there's no reason why she should. And before you ask
OF COURSE I didn't tell him about Helen — or that you and
Fiona know about it.
Reply immediately!
Tess

Hi Tess,
All OK here, just a quick update on the detective front.
Fiona's told Khaled she knows about Miriam — Why — who
knows how that girl's mind works? He might think she saw
them together on that night in London. At least you don't need
to worry that he'll think you told her. Mum says he came round
to see me — why? Please find out — that's an instruction.
More soon,
Jas xxx

I didn't know what to do after that. After a quick
mental debate I went onto *Sadiestyle*. She hadn't
changed her image since I had last looked as far as I
could see. I was reading her latest fashion post when I
realised Malika was looking over my shoulder.

'Who's she?' she asked.

'Her name's Sadie. It's a fashion blog I follow. She
lives in my town. I like her style.' Malika wrinkled her
nose.

'How old is she? My mum dresses like that.' I looked
at the outfit she was pointing to. Sara was pretty smart
looking.

'She's seventeen,' I said.

'She looks older. Show me some more images.' I
opened up a page where Sadie had the short red bob
that I had so carefully cultivated until last week.

'Her hair is awful,' said Malika, 'she's kind of plastic, don't you think? I don't mean to be rude,' she added hastily. 'What do I know about fashion?'

I looked at her. Today she was wearing skinny black trousers and a grey top, with contrasting black and grey scarf and chunky black boots and lots of heavy silver jewellery. She looked good. She had her own style. I looked back at Sadie. Maybe she wasn't quite as perfect as I had thought. I clicked the screen shut.

'Hi girls.'

We both looked up.

'Hi Papa,' said Malika.

'Can I join you?' he asked. 'Sara's gone upstairs to have a shower.'

Malika stood up.

'Don't go,' I said.

'I need to get something from my room.' She slipped past Michael. 'I won't be long.'

'Jasmine.' He cleared his throat. 'I owe you an explanation, I know. I'm pleased you seem to be getting on with Malika.'

'It makes it easier for you, doesn't it? Is that why you invited me here, hoping we'd get on and then I would forgive you everything?'

He rubbed his hands over his face.

'I understand that you're angry.'

'Angry?' I spluttered the word out. I gripped the edges of my chair, my voice rising. 'Do you know what it has been like for Mum and me? She has never hidden the truth from me – I always knew that you abandoned her when I was just a baby, but now it's even worse – it turns out that you had got another woman pregnant *at*

124

the same time! I always wanted a sister or brother.' I was shouting now. Michael looked alarmed. 'When you abandoned us you ruined her life. If only I'd known you'd swapped me for another baby then I wouldn't have bothered looking for you.'

'You looked for me?'

'Of course I did! As soon as I was old enough to understand I tried to find you. I was convinced that you had made a mistake, that something was preventing you from coming back to us. I tried for ages to work out where you might have gone but I had to give up in the end, I came to my senses and realised you didn't want me any more.' Tears were springing into my eyes now. 'You had another child that you loved more, another family. Do you know how much that hurts?' I scrunched my eyes up, determined not to let him see me cry.

'Jasmine, let me try and explain. Your mother and I were having problems; we had been for a long time. I behaved badly. Caroline refused to let me see you. Maybe I should have tried harder, but even my own mother cut me out of her life, she adored Caroline, she always had. She's never met Malika.'

'So why have you got in touch with Mum now after all this time?'

'Caroline contacted me.'

'No she didn't! She told me that you needed to get some documents from Gran.' As I was speaking I could see from his expression that Mum had lied to me. I sat back down, the breath taken out of me.

'She contacted me completely out of the blue to let me know my mother was ill. She said Mum had been talking about me, reminiscing.' I could picture the scene, Mum often started rambling down the phone after a few glasses of wine. 'Naturally I asked about you, I told her I would like to see you but she refused to talk about it. She rang me the next day and told me to forget that she had rung, but it was too late by then. I went to see Mum in the care home.' He screwed up his face. 'That was hard. I've always hoped she would agree to meet Malika but she refused. She wasn't very rational though, she was all over the place. She loves you so much, Jasmine, I think she thought she would be betraying you if she let another grandchild into her life. I know how involved she has been in your upbringing.'

'Why didn't you tell Malika about me sooner?'

'Once Sara was pregnant and I had been outcast by my family I cut off all ties. Sara knew about you of course, but she knew I didn't want to talk about it. The question of telling Malika didn't really arise. I suppose I hoped I would never have to deal with the situation. Burying my head in the sand, as usual, hoping things would go away.'

'Like telling Malika six months ago?'

'I know, I know. I always meant to tell her, but I kept putting it off and before I knew it she was a teenager already. But she's a great kid, I knew she'd look out for you; she's a very kind person.' He paused. 'Sara has had her own problems to deal with and Malika is fiercely protective of her. She must get that from her mother – it certainly doesn't come from me.'

Silence filled the room. Not an uncomfortable silence. What he had said made sense, it fitted with

126

what Mum had said about him leaving. It didn't mean I forgave him.

I felt a hand on my shoulder and Malika sat back down.

'I've been trying to apologise,' Michael said, looking at her. 'I apologise to you too, for not telling you about Jasmine earlier.'

'I forgive you,' she said, 'but you'll do it again won't you? You're always so secretive.'

'No I'm not,' he said. 'What makes you say that?'

'Like when I ask exactly what it is you do at work and you refuse to talk about it. Or what about when you went to Belgium?'

'What are you talking about?'

'The trip you went on at the end of May. You missed my birthday, remember?' Michael shifted about on his chair, then stood up. Malika carried on talking. 'You were gone longer than usual and when I asked about it you bit my head off. I wanted to know what was so important that you had to miss my birthday. I get now why you would never talk about England but it hurt me every time you shut me out. I just wanted to find out about my roots and what makes me who I am. Like Mum and her Moroccan side — I've gone really far back with my family tree for that side of the family, but I know next to nothing about you.'

Michael held his hands up in the air and went to the door. He looked like he'd rather be anywhere else. 'Girls, I'm sorry. I'll try and make it up to you, both of you.' He stood up and walked out of the room.

Malika's face was flushed. I'd never seen her so distressed before.

'Let's go out,' I said. 'Show me the area. Forget about Michael.'

She smiled ruefully. We both knew it would be impossible to think about anything else.

It was early evening and the area was buzzing. Little grocers shops with racks of colourful fruit and veg were still open, interspersed with smart clothes and jewellery shops, some of which had started the process of winding down for the evening. The tables outside the cafes were still full of people, drinking coffees and beers, heated discussions were taking place with old men in fishing jackets gesticulating at one another, smoking furiously. Buses and cars hurtled down the street and people headed purposefully towards the nearest Metro station, St Paul, disappearing down the steps into the tunnels underneath our feet.

'Would you like an ice cream?' Malika asked.

I shook my head. My throat was too tight. She linked her arm through mine.

'A drink then,' she said. She led me down a side street to a little bar with a couple of tables outside. 'You sit here,' she said. I pulled a chair sideways so that the sun's rays fell on my face, warming me outside, but having no effect on my cold insides. Michael's words were still swimming around in my head. Malika emerged with two glasses and poured us each some water from a carafe on the table.

I watched her as she carefully licked her ice cream, she was so unlike any of my friends at home.

'What are you thinking about?' she asked.

'You,' I said. 'I'm trying to understand what it must

be like for you, living with Michael, then me turning up. Are you angry with him?'

She shook her head. 'Not angry, disappointed. I wish he could have been honest with me – and Maman – all along. 'He made mistakes, yes, but it was a long time ago now.'

'How can you say that? Time doesn't mean it's any less wrong.'

She frowned. 'I meant we must put the mistakes behind us – good things have come out of it after all. I've met you.'

'I thought it would be hard for you finding out about your Grandma.'

'What do you mean?'

'Grandma taking Mum's side and refusing to see you. He said he always wanted her to meet you.' Realisation dawned on me. 'That's what Gran meant, last time I went. You're *the other one.*'

'I don't know what you are talking about. Besides, she's not related to me. There's no reason for her to want to see me.'

I stared at her. 'She's Michael's mother. Your grandmother. Our grandmother,' I added quietly.

Malika's eyes widened. 'But I thought my grandparents were dead! Isn't she your maternal grandmother?' I shook my head. 'How could he do that?' Her face seemed to fall apart.

I talked rapidly. 'Gran adored Mum and when they split up she blamed Michael completely. She took Mum's side. She knew about the other woman and refused to speak to him again. Now she has Alzheimer's and has to live in a home. Gran told me

Michael had been to see her. Sometimes now she doesn't recognise me but last time was awful. She shouted at me and said she'd told Michael that she didn't want to see me. She must have got confused and thought I was you. She screamed at me to get out... the nurse told me he'd been in to see her just the week before.' Surprise registered on Malika's face. 'I'm sorry Malika, I didn't realise you didn't know who Gran was.'

Malika was crying, her ice cream forgotten and dripping into the cornet. I took it from her and dumped the remains in the ash tray on the table and put my hand on her arm.

'Please don't cry. Gran will come round. I'll talk to her when she's having one of her lucid moments — she'll see you if I ask her — when I tell her what a lovely person you are.' A tear was threatening to emerge and I rubbed furiously at my eyes. 'I can show you a photo if you like.' I rummaged around in my bag for my phone. Malika sniffed.

'I'd like that.'

I scrolled through my photographs, looking for Gran. I wanted to find a photo that would do her justice.

'When did Papa visit her?' she asked. 'How recently was it?'

'About a month ago,' I said, calculating quickly in my head.

'But Michael hasn't been to England for years. He told me, it's taken him so long to agree to move back there. I thought you were mistaken when you mentioned it earlier.'

I closed my eyes, thinking for a moment, 'When did

Michael go to Belgium?' I asked. 'The exact date.'

'That's easy,' she said, 'it was my birthday. I was really upset that he missed my party. All my friends came and he wasn't there.'

'The date?' I reminded her.

'May 25th of course. My fourteenth birthday.'

CHAPTER 22

That was the moment I knew I had to tell her. First I gave her a handkerchief and went into the café. In schoolgirl French I think I managed to order an orange juice and a glass of white wine. The woman pointed to the table which I took to mean she would bring the drinks outside and I went back to Malika.

She looked more composed now. She was re-pinning her headscarf and managed a sort of smile. Next she picked up my phone and used it as a mirror, reapplying the smudged black kohl around her eyes.

'Better?' I asked. She nodded. The woman from the café came out at that moment carrying a tray and put our drinks, plus a tray of green olives down on the table. She tucked a piece of paper under the plate and went back inside.

'I hope you've got enough money for that,' she said. 'Is that wine?'

I nodded. 'I've got quite a few bad habits you're going to find out about sooner or later.'

She rolled her eyes. 'I guessed as much.'

I took a sip of my wine, suddenly thinking of Mum. Had she left for New York yet? I had lost track of time. Maybe she was flying over Paris right now.

'There's something I need to tell you,' I said, taking another gulp of my drink, pushing the fat green olives away. 'It's about Michael but you absolutely have to be sworn to secrecy.' She nodded. 'I mean it,' I said. 'It could have serious consequences otherwise.'

'What on earth are you talking about?' she asked.

So I told her everything. Different expressions flickered across her face as I told her what had happened since I had seen Michael on *Crimewatch*. At the first mention of the programme she sat very still. Eventually she spoke.

'I won't say anything because I absolutely know my father is innocent. He would never do anything like that. He may be a liar and a cheat but...'

'It doesn't sound too good when you put it like that,' I joked.

'...but he would never do such a terrible thing. And think about it. If he knew he was wanted in England why would he even think about moving back there? We have to find out what exactly he was doing. Why are you smiling? This isn't a funny situation.'

'I was just thinking how I had exactly the opposite reaction, but don't forget when I saw him on TV I had only just found out that Mum had been in touch with him again. Now do you understand why I wanted to meet him? I have to know why he didn't stay and speak to the police.'

'*If* it was him.'

'So what do we do now?'

'Well, we need to find out exactly what he did that weekend. Why did he say he was in Belgium? Do you think Sara would know anything? That's the first thing you can do, try and see what she knows.' I remembered the photograph. 'I also have something else I need to show you.'

'Tell me again about this boy Khaled. Do you think he is suspicious?'

'He did lie about where he was to Fiona but I don't think that counts.' Malika pulled a face. 'I don't mean his behaviour isn't wrong but I think hiding the fact that he was two-timing Fiona was his main motivation. However, according to Mark he went somewhere that weekend and came back covered in mud. Where Miriam disappeared was very muddy but so are a lot of places. We need to find out where he went that evening and why he couldn't even tell Mark.'

'Did Mark know he had another girlfriend?'

I thought for a moment. 'That's a good point. I don't know. If he did then there would be no reason not to tell him. I can find that out. Tess can ask him for me. The other thing about Michael is why did he leave the scene after finding the body? If, as you say, he is innocent, what did he not want the police to find out?'

Malika bent down and took her laptop out of her bag, then set it down on the table. 'Can you show me the *Crimewatch* footage? She opened the laptop lid, then shut it again quickly. 'This is our father we are talking about – are we really doing the right thing?'

'Yes,' I said. 'Why are we doing this?'

'I want to clear his name.'

'And I want to find out the truth.'

'You're right,' she said, 'so let's get on with it.'

We sat and watched the footage from the episode of *Crimewatch* which had turned my life upside down. I was holding my breath as it reached the moment where the photograph was shown, suddenly convinced I'd been mistaken all along. Malika gasped when she saw it, her hand flying to her mouth. She turned to me, panic in her eyes.

'It really is him! I was hoping that you were wrong but there is absolutely no doubt about that picture. Even with the beard.'

'Let me show you something else I found,' I said. I pulled out the photograph and handed it to her. 'This was the first time I saw Sara,' I said. 'I wasn't very pleased either, I'd wanted her to be horrid but she looks lovely. As she is, actually.'

Malika was staring at the photograph. 'Have you looked at this photograph since you came to Paris?' she asked.

'No, why?'

She held it out to me. 'Because this isn't my mother,' she said. 'Look closely, there's a resemblance alright but I'd know this face anywhere. This woman is my aunt.'

The colour was draining out of her face.

'What's the matter?'

'This is my aunt, Nora, my mum's sister.' She pointed at the photograph and I noticed how her hands were shaking. 'She is five years younger than my mother and she came to France from Morocco at the same time as my mother. They were very close and I know all about her, yet I have never met her. Nora disappeared before I was born.'

'What do you mean disappeared?'

She shrugged her shoulders. 'Exactly that. She vanished. She didn't turn up for work one day and has never been seen since. Maman was devastated, the whole family were. The police looked into it but you know they say she is an adult, what can they do? Where did you get this?'

'Gran had it. The nurse found it after Michael visited the care home. He must have dropped it. But at least it's quite reasonable for Michael to have this picture.' I was relieved.

'No,' she whispered, 'it's not normal at all. Look at this photo! You thought it was Maman. Nora looked much younger than this when she disappeared. This is a much more recent photo. Don't you see? This means that she is still alive! I have to go and ask Papa where he got this!'

I grabbed her arm.

'No! You can't! If you let him know we're suspicious about him he'll be on his guard all the time. Please, Malika, don't say anything, at least not for a while.'

She stared hard at the photograph, as if her gaze could bring it to life. When she looked up at me her eyelashes were wet with tears.

'I can't believe this. Maybe you're right, maybe Papa isn't so innocent after all.'

CHAPTER 23

'There's the fountain,' Malika pointed to an old monument surrounded by tourists. It was just like the one at Piccadilly Circus. 'The internet café is there, I'll meet you back here in an hour, OK?'

I nodded. Ten minutes later I was logged onto my email account. Tess had replied almost immediately to my last reply.

Hi Jas,

You won't believe how antsy Khaled has got! He cornered me and made me promise not to tell anyone about Miriam. I said of course I wouldn't (you don't count and he doesn't need to know that you know.) Mark said he seems really distracted in rehearsals, which is so out of character – he normally takes charge of the band. That girl Sadie's brother has joined the band now; in fact his whole family have gone on holiday to Ibiza and he persuaded his parents to let him stay home alone while they're away – just so he can join the band. He's a good keyboard player so Mark's pretty pleased. Talking of Mark, he keeps asking about you!!! Is there something you're not telling me?!! How's it going in Paris? Have you been up the Eiffel Tower yet?

Details please ASAP!

Tess

So Sadie was on holiday. I pushed the thought away – Sadie was out of my life now – it was ironic that she was creeping onto the edges of our investigation. I owed Tess a reply. I checked the time; I still had half an hour left, before I had to meet Malika back at the fountain.

Hi Tess,

Paris is not bad so far but I haven't climbed any towers and have no intention of doing so! I have seen the Eiffel Tower and various other famous places but it is far more interesting where the hotel is. There are cafes everywhere and the traffic is crazy; people honk their horns ALL the time. Most people speak English luckily, I never was any good at French!

My family – where to start? It was very awkward with Michael at first but some of the things I have found out about what he did make it easier. His wife Sara is OK, she's from Morocco originally, very pretty and nice so it's hard not to like her. I know you will scream loudly when you read this but I have a sister! A real half-sister and she is a Muslim! Her name is Malika and I am totally freaked out as you can imagine. We get on really well and I have told her EVERYTHING. She didn't know about me either so there is a lot of family stuff going on and lots of slamming doors, but me and Malika are sticking together. I think she can help with the Crimewatch stuff. Gotta go,

Jas xxx

Ps Quit with the matchmaking, or else….

My time was up now so I logged off and went outside into the fresh air. Tourists strolled slowly down the cobbled street, different languages floating up into the air. I turned right and made my way back to the fountain. Malika was lounging against the wall, gazing into space, her brow furrowed in concentration. I went up and tapped her on the arm, making her jump.

'Sorry,' I said. She kissed me on both cheeks, then gestured towards the river.

'Let's go this way.' She linked her arm through mine as we walked slowly past little touristy shops, full of a million different versions of the Eiffel Tower.

'I can't get Nora out of my mind. I even dreamed about her last night.'

'I thought you'd never met her?'

'I didn't, but Mum talked about her so much I always felt as if I knew her. She was very different to my mother. Mum is very serious and efficient. Nora was a bit wild. She totally rejected her religion at an early age and caused a bit of a scandal in the family by going out with a non-Muslim boy when she was about sixteen. Mum was close to her and used to pick up the pieces after her various crises. I don't think Papa liked her, he thought she was unstable and relied on Maman too much.'

We walked for a while in silence.

'Where are we going?'

'I suppose we're heading towards the hotel. Did you want to do something?'

'I wouldn't mind seeing that building you showed me the other day when we were at the top of the Pompidou Centre, the funny white one that looks like the sort of palace I read about in stories when I was little.'

'Oh you mean Sacre-Coeur! OK, let's go. I need something to take my mind off everything. We can go on the metro, it's quicker.'

We headed back towards the fountain and went down into the metro via a steep staircase. Malika pulled a couple of tickets out of her back pocket and we went through the barrier and headed down towards the platform. There was a strange smell of musty eggs down by the tracks. I wrinkled my nose and Malika started laughing. It was different from the tube in London; you could see the passengers waiting on the other side of the platform for the train going the other way. A man was strumming a guitar with a dopey looking dog at his side. The track started vibrating and people edged forward as the noise of the approaching train filled the tunnel. A man standing near to the busker looked vaguely familiar. The busker stopped playing, stood up and handed a package to the man. The dog started barking as the noise of the train approaching filled the tunnel. Malika and I looked at one another in astonishment. The man was Michael.

'Papa!' shouted Malika, before I could stop her. At that moment the train roared onto the platform in front of us, drowning out her voice. I grabbed her and we edged back towards the wall, as passengers around us pushed urgently onto the train. As the noise of the departing train filled the air I held my breath, willing the train to move out of the way. I hadn't noticed the train arriving on the other side and when my vision was clear I finally released my breath, but it was too late. The platform opposite was empty.

CHAPTER 24

'Quick!' shouted Malika and we rushed to the staircase on the side of the station and galloped up the stairs. She paused for a moment at the top then pointed to a sign saying 'Porte de Clignancourt' and raced towards it. She was fast and I cursed myself for wearing heels, they weren't that high but I hadn't anticipated racing around a tube station when I chose my clothes this morning. Malika's boots were far better suited to the occasion. I couldn't help running into her with a thump as she came to a sudden stop at the edge of the platform.

'They won't be here now,' I gasped. 'They must have got on the train.' We both scanned the platform, which was slowly filling up with passengers again, but the busker and dog had gone. And there was definitely no sign of Michael.

'Let's go back upstairs,' I suggested. 'We don't know for sure whether Michael got on the train.'

We retraced our steps, Malika rooting around in her bag and pulling out her phone.

'You have a quick look around,' she said, 'I'm making a call.' I wandered up and down the platform, but I was convinced Michael had jumped on the train

Malika came back over to me. 'That was Maman,' she said. 'I asked her where Papa was working today. She said he had a meeting out of town, he won't be back until this evening. And he took the car.'

'You didn't say anything did you?'

'Of course I didn't! But what happened there? What is he up to?'

'It was him, wasn't it?

'I think I'd know my own father,' she said.

'Well some of us aren't so fortunate,' I muttered.

'Jasmine,' she grabbed my arm, 'you know I didn't mean anything by it. I'm wondering who that man was.'

'Well we'll never know now will we.'

Malika and I separated when we got back to the hotel. I thought she'd forgotten to tell me something when there was a knock at my door. I was surprised to see Sara standing outside.

'Can I talk to you?' she asked. Her smile was warm, so like Malika's. She followed me into the room and sat down at the desk. 'I thought we should get to know one another. You are my husband's daughter after all and my own daughter is very fond of you already, I can tell. Are you missing your mother?'

I shook my head. 'Mum's got a very high-powered job. She works long hours.' A picture of Mum sprang into my head, glass of wine in hand, talking to Clare on the phone. 'Even when she gets home from work, which is late, she carries on working. I don't mind, though,' I added, 'we get on great. Do you have a big family?'

'My parents live in Morocco and I have two sisters

142

and two brothers.'

'In France?' I asked.

She looked sad. 'My brother Ali lives in Lille. My little sister also used to live there too, but I don't see her any more. She went missing a few years ago and we never found out what happened to her.'

'That's terrible. Are you still looking for her?'

She smiled sadly. 'Every time I go out of the house I am scanning the streets with my eyes to see if I can see her, I refuse to believe I will never see her again.'

'That's how I felt about my dad when I was little,' I said quietly, 'I always expected him to call me, or send me a card on my birthday. Every night when I got home from school I waited.'

'I understand.' She patted my hand and I didn't mind. 'It's the not knowing that is so hard. If I knew she had chosen to leave us and she was OK then I could let it go, but...' at that moment Malika pushed the door open.

'Can I come in?' She stood behind her mum and put her arms around her neck. 'What are you two talking about?' she asked.

'I was just telling Jasmine about Aunty Nora.' Jasmine looked at me in alarm over her mother's head. I shook my head very slightly. She relaxed.

'Have you heard from Papa today?' she asked, sitting down on the bed.

'He rang this afternoon and said the meeting was going well.' she laughed. 'We're all going out for dinner later.'

'I'd better have a shower then,' I said.

'Come on, Malika, let's give Jasmine a bit of peace.'

143

I pulled the photo of Nora out of the zipped pocket in my bag and studied the pretty face. What had happened to her? I lay back on the bed and closed my eyes. Moments later I was asleep, Malika, Sara and Michael were running around the Paris metro in my dreams, while I tried desperately to keep up with them, a dog snapping at my heels.

A hand was on my shoulder, shaking me. I opened my eyes.

'It's time to eat,' said Malika.

Sara and Michael were waiting outside their room. As we listened to the grinding sound of the lift approaching, my nose started itching. I sneezed loudly.

'Oh no,' I groaned. 'I always sneeze at least five times and I haven't got a tissue.'

'Take this,' said Sara, handing me the passkey to her room. 'There's a pack on the table.' A loud ping announced the arrival of the lift. 'We'll wait for you downstairs.'

I let myself into the room and spotted the tissues straight away on the table. I sneezed four times. As I blew my nose loudly I noticed Michael's battered leather case by the side of the bed. An image of the man holding the case on the station platform flashed through my head. Without stopping to think, I unclasped the catch and opened the case. My hands trembled slightly as I saw the package straight away. This had to be it! It was a large padded envelope. It had been opened already and I put my trembling hand in and pulled out a few sheets of papers. I glanced at the door, but the corridor was silent. I had to be quick.

The documents were in French. I pulled out my phone and took close-up shots of each piece of paper on both sides. I shoved the envelope back in the case, grabbed the rest of the tissues and ran out into the corridor.

They were standing in the foyer, and Michael stepped forward when he saw me, as if to give me a hug but I swerved him.

'Sorry I took so long, 'I said.

Sara smiled. 'Malika always sneezes a hundred times too.'

'How was your day in Paris?' Michael asked. 'Is Malika looking after you?'

'Yes,' I said.

'We saw someone who looked just like you on the platform at St Michel, Papa,' said Malika, 'talking to a busker.' I watched Michael carefully. Surprise flickered across his face, before he quickly turned his head away.

'A lookalike!' he said. 'I was out in the car today. Let's go, we don't want to miss our reservation at the restaurant.'

Malika looked at me. I could read the dismay in her eyes. I squeezed her arm as we walked behind Sara and Michael into the restaurant.

CHAPTER 25

After dinner I waited until Michael and Sara were safely in their room, before tapping on Malika's door.

'Malika, are you awake?'

'I am now,' she said. She was wearing a long t-shirt with pyjama bottoms and her curls cascaded over her shoulders.

'I'm scared,' she said. 'Every now and then I remember the photograph of Aunty Nora that was in Papa's wallet. It's really hard not to say anything, you saw how Maman is about her still, after so much time. Well it's understandable. But what if Dad did have something to do with her disappearance? Why so many secrets? He's keeping something from us and I don't like that.'

My eyes were becoming accustomed to the dark. Malika pulled herself up so that she was leaning her head against the headrest. Her eyes glinted in the dark, the streetlights casting shadows across the room. Every now and then a car purred by.

'It was him, though, wasn't it, at St Michel? Or was I seeing things?'

I took my phone out of my dressing gown. 'It was definitely him. I've got proof.'

'What do you mean?' Her eyes were large and round.

'His case was in the room when I went to get the tissues. I looked inside.'

'Jasmine! You shouldn't have done that.'

'How else are we supposed to find out what's going on?'

'We could ask him.'

'Yeah right, and let him know that we're onto him. Then he'll be extra careful. You want to prove him innocent don't you?'

She bit down on her lip. 'I suppose so. Let's see then, what have you got?'

I handed her my phone and showed her the shots I'd taken of the papers. Her dark eyes scanned back and forth. She cried out, clapping her hand to her mouth.

'What is it?' I asked. She looked up at me, and with a shock I realised that her eyes were brimming with tears.

'It's Nora's birth certificate,' she said. 'Why does he have this? What is he up to?'

'What are the others?'

She didn't move for a moment. She was still scanning the text, disbelief written across her face. She shook her head, then clicked onto the next photo.

'How many more are there?'

'Two.' Her hands were trembling slightly as she held the second up to read.

'What is it?'

'It's a reference for Nora, written by...' she squinted at the signature and swiped the screen to make it larger.

147

'I can't read the writing at all, wait…oh it's printed here. A Marc Dupont from the Hotel Président in Lille.' She shrugged. 'Then this last one is a list of job vacancies, all in the hotel trade and all in England.' She looked up at me. 'Nora must be in England, she has to be.'

'Let me see that list,' I held out my hand. An idea was forming. I scanned the list of hotels, all of which were in towns around the south of England. I jabbed my finger at the text, there it was, what I had been looking for.

'The Hotel Metropole, Amersham.' Malika was looking quizzically at me. 'That's where Michael stayed when he was in England. Maybe Nora is working there and he went to see her?'

Malika was shaking her head. 'I can't believe he knows where she is. He knows how desperate Maman is for information. Jasmine, I think we have to tell her, speak to Papa. I don't think I can bear keeping secrets from her.'

'You can't,' I pleaded. 'Think about it. If you tell Sara then she will insist on speaking to Michael about it. If he knows what we suspect, he can lie and cover up what he is doing. If he is guilty, and don't forget there is the crucial problem of what his connection with Miriam is, then he can make it very difficult for us to find out the truth.'

Malika looked miserable. 'The best thing,' I continued, clutching at the right thing to say, 'Is that we carry on trying to find out what happened when we get back to England.'

'I guess so,' Malika asked. She didn't look too happy

. 'Can we visit this hotel?'

I nodded. 'Definitely.'

Malika yawned. 'I need to get some sleep.'

'First thing tomorrow I'm going to check my emails and see if Tess has got any news from back home. I haven't seen any English newspapers, so I don't know what's going on with the police and Miriam. They may have found more details.'

I was up early the next morning, and after snatching a croissant from the breakfast bar, I went straight to the public internet point. I logged straight into my email account. There was an email from Tess.

'OMG,' was the subject. I smiled, typical drama queen Tess.

You won't believe what has been happening here! I have only had four hours sleep due to extensive investigations carried out last night. Josh (remember he is Sadie's brother who has joined Mark's band) threw a party at his place as his folks are still away. I went with Mark and the rest of the guys from the band (yes including Khaled cos I know you're wondering.) The house is AMAZING and he had invited loads of fit boys from his college. MORE OF THAT LATER. Melanie Moore and her stuck up friends were all there ignoring me but not being as blatant as usual because I gained a bit of street cred being with Mark and the band. Khaled was still being weird with me (Fiona wasn't there) and he kept coming over and asking me not to say anything about Miriam. I got fed up with it in the end and suggested maybe he had something to hide. He was a bit pissed and got really angry with me and started yelling and Mark and Josh had to pull him away from me. Mark made me

149

tell him what we were arguing over, he threatened to tell Mum I'd been at the party if I didn't fess up. Anyhow I'm afraid Mark knows everything. Des took Khaled outside and managed to calm him down and persuaded him to leave as Josh was about to call the police. Mark is furious at what we've been up to and he says he's going to speak to Khaled and find out what's really going on.

So if that wasn't enough excitement, Josh, who is EVER so slightly gorgeous spent the rest of the evening looking after me and...wait for it....he asked me out at the end of the evening. Oh, and he kissed me.... OMGGG!!! So that's why I didn't sleep at all and I don't think I ever will again and obviously you must be thinking that I will never wash my cheek again – but it wasn't a kiss on the cheek – It was a proper steamy SNOG!!

Can't wait to chat,
Love Tess xxx

Tess was always having adventures. She hadn't mentioned Miriam, so I googled her name to look through the latest newspaper stories. I spotted Malika heading towards me.

'You're keen,' she said, 'budge up.' She squashed onto the seat beside me. I inhaled a citrusy perfume. Today she was wearing all black, her eyes rimmed with heavy black kohl and silver eye shadow. So different from Sadie. I realized with a jolt that I had barely given her a thought since I arrived in Paris.

'Read that,' I said, finishing off my croissant while she read the article. Flakes of pastry scattered all over my lap, and I brushed them away, listening as Malika read aloud.

There has been an overwhelming response to last week's Crimewatch appeal concerning murdered teenager Miriam Jackson, in particular regarding the missing witness who reported the finding of the body to police. Sightings have reportedly been made in York, Madrid, Edinburgh and the Isle of Wight.

She stopped reading. 'Not Paris, then. 'I can't believe nobody has recognized him. I suppose if it had happened in France…'

I nudged her. 'Carry on.'

CCTV footage captured Miriam's last movements at Marylebone station, but there are no cameras at Keston. Police are believed to know the identity of Miriam's boyfriend, but his name has not been made public at present.

'Does that mean they know about Khaled?' Malika asked.

I shrugged. 'Who knows? If I was him I'd hand myself in, clear my name.'

'Unless…' I didn't want to go there.

'Hi girls.'

The baritone voice made me jump and Malika closed the web page down and logged off.

'You don't have to stop.' Michael was wearing jeans and a t-shirt and his hair was damp. 'Sara wants you to go shopping with her, Malika, help her buy a present for your cousin. So I thought I'd take Jasmine out on the Bateaux Mouches.'

I looked up at him. 'What's that?'

'The tourist boat, the one I showed you on the river,' said Malika. 'You'll love it.'

'Don't you want to come?'

'I promised Maman I'd help her. She has no idea what to get Chloe. You go with dad.'

'It's our last day,' he said, 'and we haven't spent much time together have we? Malika has been keeping you all to yourself.' He smiled, but sounded nervous.

'OK,' I said. The boat would be fun, and I didn't have to talk to him.

We sat up on the deck, a breeze blowing through my hair and I breathed deeply. Michael handed me a can of coke and sat down next to me. I sat slightly at a distance from him. We opened our drinks and I took a long mouthful. The cold liquid tasted delicious.

The commentary drifted across me, I tuned into the English descriptions of ancient bridges and buildings every now and then. I studied Michael, still uncomfortable. He was in good shape for an oldie. He wasn't bad looking and in different circumstances I would have been proud that he was my dad. He looked across at me.

'I will make things up to you Jas.'

'Is it true that you wanted to keep in touch with me?'

'Honestly, Jasmine, I swear on Malika's life.'

'Mum said the same thing,' I said quietly. He reached over and took my hand. I let him. His hand felt strong and warm, protective.

'It broke my heart to leave you, not to see you grow up, your first words, your first steps, all those important landmarks in your life that I missed out on.'

I sighed. 'You could have stayed in touch, Christmas, birthdays.' The boat sailed under another bridge. There were tents on the embankment, a dog tied to a post.

'I had little choice. My own mother was taking Caroline's side. The stress was making me ill; I had to get on with my life. I thought about you every day, Jasmine.'

He was squeezing my hand with emotion and I realised with horror that he had tears in his eyes. 'Could we start again do you think?'

'What do you mean?'

'Put the past behind us. A new beginning. Now that I've found you again, I don't want to lose you.'

My stomach was churning inside. His words were taking my heartstrings and twisting them, but I couldn't stop thinking about all that other stuff I knew about him. How could I make a fresh start when all the time I was investigating him?

'Eh Jasmine, what do you say?'

I was glad I still had shades on to hide my eyes behind. I didn't want him to see my dilemma. I nodded.

The boat drifted along past more impressive buildings on the banks, and I tuned back into the commentary, Michael pointing out the odd landmark.

'Michael,' I said

'Yes?'

'I would like to come back to Amersham with you, stay for a few days. As long as I won't get in the way of your move.'

His mouth twitched at the corners. He didn't need to answer.

I felt lighter as we entered the hotel. Getting to know Michael was complicating my theories. I chewed on my lip. *Could he possibly be innocent?* I was starting to hope so. The ringtone of Michael's phone interrupted my thoughts. He stopped to take the call.

'Sara? Sara calm down, what is it? OK, I'm in the foyer now, I'm coming up.'

He turned to me, his face pale and etched with worry.

'Something terrible has happened.' Bypassing the lift, he bounded towards the staircase and hurtled through the door, leaving it swinging behind him. *Not Malika?* I thought, and charged after him.

CHAPTER 26

Sara was sobbing in her hotel room, Malika at her side. I loitered in the doorway, my heart rate slowing down to a more normal level. She rushed over and threw her arms around Michael and spoke rapidly in French. I hovered around the doorway, feeling like a big fat gooseberry. Malika came outside and closed the door behind her.

'What's happened?'

The police called to tell her there had been an accident. In Lille. It's her brother Ali. He's been in a car crash and . . .' she stifled a sob and wiped at her nose. 'He's dead. He drove into a tree. There were no witnesses, so we won't know any more until the police have investigated.' She sank to the floor and I sat beside her.

'Are you close to him?'

He shook his head. 'No, I haven't seen him for ages, but it's still a shock. Mum has a friend in Lille and she usually goes to see him when she's staying with her. He lives on his own.'

'Would you like some tea? Mum always says tea is good for shock.'

Malika managed a smile. 'That's very English. I'll stay here,' she said.

I took the lift and went out of the hotel. There was

a McDonalds around the corner and it was easier for me to buy stuff from there. I stood outside and gulped down some fresh air. A feeling of aloneness had descended on me.

Malika was still sitting outside the room when I got back. I put the tea down next to her and took the other two cups inside. Sara was sitting with her back to the door. I pulled the door to behind me and sat down next to Malika.

'I'm upset for Maman. I can't bear to see her so sad. I think at times like this she misses Nora more than ever.'

'Aren't the rest of her family in Morocco?'

She nodded. 'Nora and Ali came over here together. Nora used to live in Lille, before she went missing. Ali used to visit more often when Nora was around, but he stopped coming so much after that.'

'He must have missed her terribly too.'

She nodded. 'I suppose so.'

Michael came back out. 'Malika, can you come in here a moment? Sorry Jasmine, we won't be long.'

'That's OK,' I said. 'I'm going downstairs for a bit.'

Sadiestyle hadn't been updated since I last looked. That was unusual. I logged onto my email to have a look at Sadie's account. The password was rejected. My skin felt hot. I tried it again, making sure to correctly type the letters. A message flashed up:

Password changed two days ago

Anxiety hit me like a punch. I took some deep

breaths. Had she found out I'd been hacking into her account? I clicked backed onto her fashion blog and looked at her photograph. I thought back to what Malika and Mark had both said about my hair. Red didn't suit me. I wondered if she was back from Ibiza, then I stopped myself. I was supposed to be forgetting Sadie.

Someone tapped me on the shoulder. It was Michael. I minimized the screen.

'How is Sara?' I asked.

'She's OK,' he said. 'We'll have to go to Lille. I'm going to drive her there in the morning. There's not much she can do tonight. The police want her to identify the body and I think she would be better having a night's sleep to prepare herself.'

'If she can sleep,' I said. He looked at me.

'I'm sorry your stay has been so short,' he said. 'We need a long while to get to know each other again but I think we had just about made a start, don't you?'

'Yeah.' My voice sounded gruff. 'What about Malika?'

He sighed. 'Sara doesn't want her to go to Lille. She thinks it will be too upsetting for her. I'll be coming back to England but not for a day or so. We haven't worked out what to do yet.'

'She can come back with me! We can stay with Mark, he wont mind, honestly, and Mum will be back mid-week. Then we can come back to Amersham together.' I looked at him, willing him to say yes.

'Are you sure? That might work. We can drop you off at the station on our way to Lille. I'll give Caroline a ring, let her know what's going on.' He pulled up a

157

chair next to me. 'How is your mother? I know I have no right to ask, but I would like to know.'

I sighed. 'She's OK. She works too hard but she has friends.'

'What about you, do you have friends?'

'Tess is my best friend, but she doesn't live near me any more. She's back for the summer though, which is why I wanted to stay at her brother's. She'll love Malika.'

It felt OK, talking to Michael, letting him take a few steps into my life. 'How long will you stay in Lille?'

'I'll get Sara settled in – she can stay with Chantal for as long as she needs. To be honest, I think it will do her good. It helps having Malika sorted actually, it will help take her mind off everything and Sara won't have to worry about her.'

'So when will you be coming?'

'I don't know for sure. I have some business in England next Friday. I'll let you know.' He pushed the chair back. 'I'd better go and see how Sara is. I need to help her pack.'

As I watched him go I felt a little warm glow inside me. Then I remembered. *Crimewatch*. That picture sprang into my mind every time I had a good thought about Michael. I was going to have to prove his innocence and the sooner I did it the better.

CHAPTER 27

'Don't you just love English weather,' announced Malika. The train had just emerged from the Eurotunnel and was speeding through the British countryside, sheets of rain lashing against the windows. My phone beeped as soon as I switched it back on. A text from Mum.

Arriving back on Monday. I'll text you flight times later when I can find them.

I showed Malika.

'Doesn't it bother you? Has she always been so vague?'

A picture of Mum, bottle of wine in hand framed in the kitchen doorway at home sprang into my mind. I looked away.

'What is it?'

'I think Mum drinks too much,' I said quietly. Saying it aloud felt like I was releasing a burst of air.

'I don't mean she staggers around the streets with a bottle under her arm, shouting at people, she goes to work and does normal things, she just drinks too much, that's all.'

'Does she get violent?'

'No, never! It's not like that, It's hard to explain, but I don't remember a day ever, when she didn't have a drink.'

'Maman has the odd glass of wine with dinner, she's not the best example of a good Muslim.'

'When did you start wearing a headscarf?'

'When I was ten. Mum used to talk about Aunt Nora a lot. I hated seeing her so unhappy and every day I prayed for her to feel better. I started reading about Islam more and that's when I decided. I feel more comfortable wearing my scarf, protected somehow.'

'There are a few Muslim girls at my school and they all wear it, it's part of the uniform. And forget what I just said — about her drinking I mean. You're not worried about coming now are you? Mum's alright really, and she won't care what you you wear.'

'She won't be expecting someone like me though, will she?'

Malika was dozing with her head against the window. I opened her laptop to look at my emails. Tess and Fiona had both written to me.

Hi Jas,

I so wish you were here! Mark is furious because Khaled hasn't been to band practice since the row at the party — I know he blames you — so I'm keeping out of his way as much as I can. But I don't care about any of that because Josh is now MY BOYFRIEND!!! He is adorable and I can't wait for you to meet him properly. We've been hanging out at his place — would you believe they have a swimming pool! I don't want his family ever to come back from holiday so that we can hang out here together for the rest of the summer. I'm trying to persuade him to have a pool party but he's not convinced...yet!

As regards the other stuff: I asked Fiona about information

160

on Khaled — see her response below. I haven't heard from Helen but Fiona has been in touch with her.

Bad news about Sara's brother, but it means I get to see you sooner . . .

Love Tess xxxxx

Fiona's email followed on:

Hi Tess,

This is what I know about Khaled. He is a RAT. His mum lives up North and he won't talk about her — he stays with a foster family now. I asked him once about his dad — big mistake. No sisters and brothers, he's got a cousin. He lives in one of those flats up by our old school with his foster mum. He's very protective of her — he got into a fight once when one of his friends dissed her. I haven't spoken to him since we split and I hope I never see him again.

Helen said the police have been back to see her and said they know more about the boyfriend now, but she still made out she didn't know what his name was. Let me know when Jasmine is back.

Fiona.

That was the second example of Khaled losing his temper. And he obviously hadn't had an easy childhood.

I sent Tess a text to tell her we were on our way home. She replied straight away.

At last! Josh is having another party tomorrow night.

So Sadie still wasn't home. It was hard to stop

tracking her when her brother was now involved with Tess. I tried logging into her account again but the password had definitely been changed. A cold feeling crept through my stomach, it looked like I wasn't going to have any choice. Determined now I logged onto Facebook. With disbelief I stared at the screen. Sadie had changed her status to single. Quickly I clicked on her 'friends' page. AJ was no longer there. What had happened in Ibiza?

I closed the laptop down and shut my eyes, my head propped against the headrest.

The train arrived at St Pancras on time and as we were lugging our cases through the barrier, a voice called out my name.

'Tess!' I screamed. Tess and Mark were waving a large piece of cardboard in the air. 'Jasmine and Malika' was written in large letters. Tess stood out in orange today – a floaty top and a swirly skirt. A whoosh of emotion overwhelmed me. I hugged Tess and grinned awkwardly at Mark who was standing behind her.

'This is Malika, my sister,' I said proudly. She let go of her case and proceeded to give Tess and then Mark two kisses each. Mark took our cases and led the way through the station, where a car was parked.

'It's Mark's,' said Tess. 'He passed his test last year. I didn't think we'd make it – I had to persuade him to drive as fast as possible ...' she paused to wink at me, 'but he didn't need much persuading.'

I pretended I hadn't noticed. Tess and I jumped into the back of the car, letting Malika have the front seat. Mark sped off with a screech of tyres just as a traffic warden appeared and was about to tap the car registration number into his machine.

'Lucky,' said Mark, 'that would have cost me a fortune.'

Tess bombarded Malika with questions. As we neared home I turned to Tess.

'You've been very good,' I said, 'you haven't mentioned lover boy once.'

'Oh you mean Josh,' she said, her face coming to life, 'Josh with the ripped muscles and the chiselled cheekbones, my boyfriend Josh.' She giggled loudly.

'Please Tess,' said Mark, 'you're putting me off my driving. I'm glad you're back Jasmine,' he said and I ignored Tess who was digging me in the ribs. 'She's been unbearable since she met him, maybe you can talk some sense into her.'

'Is he still in your band?' I asked.

He nodded. 'Khaled's back too. I had to do a lot of grovelling on Tess's behalf, but I persuaded him to stop being an idiot.'

'Stop exaggerating,' Tess said. 'You know he was in the wrong.' I prodded her and gave her a warning look. I didn't want her drawing any more attention to Khaled than was necessary. Mark caught my eyes in the mirror and gestured with his head towards Malika, she was fast asleep. After that we all kept quiet and watched first the sun and then a rainbow emerge over the shiny wet streets. I was glad to be back after all and even gladder that Mum wouldn't be home for a while. Mark unloaded the car while Tess showed us to our room.

'You'll have to share, I'm afraid.' It was a small room with one single bed. 'There's a camp bed underneath the bed,' she said.

'Are you both up for coming to see Mark's band tonight? It's in the hall down the road. Then there's Josh's party tomorrow night?'

Malika's eyes had widened.

'Can we go?' she asked.

'Of course,' I said. 'We can do what we like now.' At the mention of the party all my earlier resolve had disappeared. Whether Malika wanted to go or not there was no way I was going to miss the opportunity to snoop around Sadie's house.

Tess left us alone to have a rest.

'We will spend time looking for Nora won't we?' Malika looked concerned.

'Of course we will. I'm sure everything is linked, only I can't see how exactly – yet.'

It was going to be a busy weekend.

CHAPTER 28

The hall was adjacent to a busy pub. Chairs were lined up around the edges of the room, and a few tables were scattered here and there. There was a counter at one end opposite the stage, which Josh had turned into a makeshift bar. Choice was limited to beer or coke. I bought a can of each and took them back to the table where Malika was sitting. Bits of yellowing sellotape and blutak clung to scraps of paper all over the wall from previous gatherings. Despite the old and tired décor it felt good to be somewhere so familiar.

Malika and I were the first ones there.

'How was Sara?' I asked. 'You were a long time on the phone.'

'I was worried that she was regretting letting me come to England, that she would have preferred me to stay with her, but it seems to be the opposite. She says she is relieved I am here with you so that she can concentrate on sorting out everything with Uncle Ali.'

'She doesn't want you to get upset, that's all.'

The band had started setting up on stage. Mark appeared, dragging some heavy equipment behind him. He stopped when he saw me and came bounding over.

'I'm so glad you could make it.'

I shrugged. 'Malika wanted to see what a real live English band was like. Thanks for letting us stay, by the way.'

'No worries. I'll chat to you later, we need to set up. I'll be interested to know what you think.'

He continued dragging the equipment across the stage. I noticed Khaled was on stage now. I hoped there wasn't going to be any trouble.

The room quickly started filling up and I went and got a couple more cans in case they ran out. Tess arrived with Josh. It was the first time I had seen them together. He was all in black, t shirt and jeans and his blonde hair was spiked up into points with gel. He didn't look happy though, in fact Tess looked like she was giving him a lecture. He gave Tess a quick kiss before he made his way over to the stage to join the rest of the band.

'Is he alright?' I asked Tess as she came over. She frowned.

'It's his family. Even though they're miles away they're still getting to him. His sister's split with her boyfriend and she keeps phoning Josh up. Honestly, she treats him like a therapist. There's more to it than that, though.' She narrowed her eyes. 'There's something he's not telling me.'

'It all sounds a bit heavy,' I said. Malika appeared beside us and started chatting to Tess. My mind was racing at the news about Sadie, when I heard a voice saying my name. I looked round. It was Fiona.

'Hey,' I said. She nodded at me.

'Do you want to sit down?' I asked. Her hair was swept up on the back of her head and she was wearing a denim dress and high sandals. She sat down in the seat next to me and pointedly turned her back to the

166

stage. Things obviously weren't any better with Khaled.

'How's it going?' I asked.

'Who's that?' She indicated Malika, who was deep in conversation with Tess.

'She's my sister.'

'Sister?' Fiona spluttered.

'It's a long story,' I said.

'You didn't reply to my email. I thought we were supposed to be working together?'

'There was a lot of stuff going on which I didn't expect. Family stuff, you know. It's not every day you find out you have a sister.' Bubbles of irritation were starting to fizz in my stomach. 'Tess told me about the party and the row with Khaled. Has anything else happened with you? Or Helen?'

She stared at Malika. 'How can she be your sister? Oh whatever, I don't really care.' She swigged from her beer. 'Helen's mum phoned. She's worried about Helen. She's been having nightmares. Her aunt was puzzled by why she only wants to see us. I think it's because Helen's hoping we will find out what happened to Miriam. Some chance!'

Tess sat down next to us.

'Malika's gone to the loo,' she said. The band were still warming up on stage, the crowd lively now. I recognised a few faces from school, but there were lots of people I had never seen before.

'What can we do?' said Fiona. 'Has anything else happened?' I told her what Tess had told me about Khaled at the party. Fiona nodded her eyes scanning the room behind me. We'd been talking for a while and Malika hadn't returned. 'Where's Malika?' I stood up and looked over towards the toilets.

'She's there,' Tess pointed in the direction of the stage. 'And look who she's talking to.'

I followed her gaze. Malika and Khaled were standing together at the side of the stage. Fiona bristled beside me. I hoped she wasn't going to cause a scene.

'I'll go get her,' I said. I hurried over to Malika. Khaled saw me approaching and said something, they both turned around.

'I wondered where you'd got to,' I said. 'Is he bothering you?'

'Relax Jasmine man. You never told me you had a sister.' Khaled was also wearing a black shirt and black jeans, obviously some kind of uniform adopted by the band. I had to admit he looked good. He was looking from me to Malika, his eyes moving back and forth. At that moment Des came over.

'Khaled, we're on now.'

'Right,' he said, 'one minute.' He beckoned me over. 'I need to speak to you. Meet me in the interval. Outside, OK?' Next minute the lights were turned down and the deep throbbing sound of the music started up. I took Malika's arm and led her back over to our table. Fiona's glare was steely through her thick black fake lashes. I ignored her and sat down with Malika.

'He was nice,' she said.

'Do you realise who he is?' She shook her head.

'That's Khaled,' I hissed.

She stared at me. 'No way! He's really nice.'

'What did he say?'

'Nothing much, he asked who I was, how long was I here for. He's not how I expected. He looks familiar somehow. Where are his parents from?'

'I don't know. He wants to speak to me in the interval. Fiona will really like that. You remember she split up with him recently, so she's a bit touchy around him. I'm surprised she's here actually.'

'Can we go and watch the band now?' asked Malika.

'Well don't expect too much,' I said. 'Let's join Tess over there.'

We pushed through the crowd who were gathered round the stage, cans in hand, dancing to the music. I felt relaxed, my third beer slipping down easily now, the music pulsing deep inside me. It was good to be home. I watched Malika out of the corner of my eye, she was clearly enjoying herself. I shouted in Tess's ear, telling her about Khaled.

'Look after Malika when I go outside will you?' She nodded, still singing along.

'Josh is great isn't he?'

'How's it going with you two — apart from the counseling sessions?'

A big smile lit up her face. 'Great. I really like him and he says he likes me too. Can you believe that? We have a lot of fun. Too bad his family are due back soon.'

'When?' I asked.

'Sometime next week. I'm not looking forward to it — they probably won't approve of me. You should see the amount of stuff his sister has, clothes, perfume, shoes. She actually has a room just for her clothes! Josh isn't like that at all, he's really down to earth.' I rolled my eyes at her, although I was thrilled to hear about Sadie's bedroom; I had pictured it so many times before. Maybe I could even get to see it?

'Sorry, I know I can't stop talking about him. How about you? How did it go with your Dad?'

'It was getting better actually. He was trying and I was starting to understand why he left.'

We listened to a few more songs, then Mark announced that the band were taking a short break.

'Don't go away,' he announced to the room, before bounding off the stage. Tess and Malika headed off to get some more drinks and I wandered outside. I wondered where Fiona had got to; I hadn't seen her for a while.

It was dark now, so I stood in an area which was lit up by the street lamp. Should I be wary of Khaled? The door swung open throwing a burst of laughter and music into the air. A shape appeared silhouetted in the doorway, becoming Khaled as he wandered over to me, pausing to light a cigarette. The glow illuminated his face momentarily. He blew a stream of smoke into the air as he came towards me. I turned my nose up.

'Gross,' I said, 'watch where you're puffing that thing. What do you want?'

He smoked silently, flicking constantly at the butt of his cigarette.

'I heard about the party,' I said.

'So you know about me and Miriam?' he asked.

I nodded. 'Is that why you attacked Tess?'

'I didn't attack her....well I didn't mean to. I was wound up and the police had been round questioning me and I thought she must have told them something.

Now I realise it was Fiona all along. What did I ever see in her? Getting back at me like that could put me in jail.' He took a long drag of his cigarette.

'It wasn't Fiona.' I said quietly. He looked at me, his eyes boring into mine.

'So who was it then?' he asked.

'I can't tell you but it was nobody you know.' No way was he going to hear Helen's name from me.

'Jasmine, give me a break.' He threw his cigarette butt to the floor and ground it out aggressively with his foot. 'The police came to see me. Again. I came clean. I told them I went out with Miriam and everything that happened.'

'Which is?'

'I saw her on the Saturday night when she was on that course. I walked her back to her hotel, only I couldn't go right to the door in case Fiona saw me. I dropped her at the corner of the street, just round from Euston road. She was supposed to text me the next day if she had a chance to meet up with me again. It never happened. That was the last time I saw her.'

'Is that what you told the police?'

He nodded. He looked tired, his eyes heavy.

'So there's nothing you haven't told them?'

'Nothing, I swear. My girlfriend has been murdered and I couldn't tell anybody.' His voice caught in his throat. 'It's hard, man. I've been all over the place. I'm sorry I had a go at Tess, it's not her fault.'

'Have you told her that?'

He shook his head. 'I'll talk to her. Are you coming to the party tomorrow?' He nodded. 'Maybe you can speak to her then?'

171

'Yeah. I like that idea.' He glanced at his watch. 'I need to get back.'

A loud rustling sound behind me made us both turn round. The yard was empty. Khaled's eyes narrowed, glinting in the dark. I followed him towards the door, the noise from inside welcoming now. He paused at the door.

'Your sister, Malika, is she coming tomorrow?'

'Yes,' I replied.

'Cool,' he said and went inside. I noticed he had developed a spring in his step. I sighed and followed him in. Why did I have a bad feeling about this?

CHAPTER 29

Malika cooked a delicious meal before we went out the next evening. It made a change from grabbing a sandwich, or the remains of whatever happened to be in the fridge. We'd had the place to ourselves as Mark had stayed with Des, and Tess had left for Josh's this morning. Malika was in the shower and I helped myself to a beer from the fridge. My phone beeped, it was a text from Fiona:

Are you going to the party?
I replied: *Yes!*
Are you at Mark's?
Yes.
I'm on my way.

I liked the way she didn't give me a choice. It wasn't long before the doorbell rang for the second time and I got up to let her in. Her hair was loose tonight, very straight and she was wearing amazing heels.

'Nice hair,' she smirked, looking at my head. I ran my fingers through my hair. It was sticking out at funny angles. It had been hidden under a hat last night. Malika was still getting ready. I couldn't be bothered to make much effort. My jeans were clean and I was wearing a new sweatshirt I'd bought in Paris – that would have to do. I offered Fiona a drink. She declined. I poured myself another and put some music on. I was getting in the party mood.

'So what did Khaled want last night?'

'He told me what happened with Miriam the last time he saw her.' I repeated what he had told me.

'I bet he made that up,' she said, scowling.

'Why?'

'You know why. He's a liar.'

'Look, I know he's hurt you but I believed him. He looked really upset when he talked about Miriam, how hard it was for him because he couldn't tell anyone.'

'Did he say anything else?'

'No,' I said.

'Liar!' she spat out the word.

'What's the matter with you? I told you what he said.'

'You didn't say what he said about apologising to Tess.'

'Oh that, I forgot. Hang on, how do you know.... it was you wasn't it? You were listening in last night! I thought I heard something. What's the matter with you? Get out of here now if you don't trust me.'

Fiona hung her head. 'Alright, I thought you were still hiding stuff from me and I wanted to be sure.'

'Have you forgotten what I said yesterday already? There's a lot of family stuff going on that's all. I told you what happened at the parties. If we're not honest with each other and what we find out then we'll never discover what's happened. I think Khaled was telling the truth. If you can't get over him then maybe we should carry on without you. Why are you going to the party anyway? Isn't it difficult seeing him all the time?'

'Why should I stop going out because of him? I

want him to see me and realise what he's missing.' She tossed back her hair; she had clearly spent ages getting ready. Now I knew why.

At that moment Malika came in, the raised voices must have attracted her.

'Remember Fiona?' I asked.

Fiona glared at Malika. I turned on her. 'Malika spoke to Khaled last night, that's all. One conversation. No big deal. She also spoke to Tess and Josh and Mark – do you see how ridiculous you are being?'

'OK, OK,' said Fiona. 'I get it. Hi.'

Malika smiled. 'I like your dress Fiona. Shall we go?' Fiona attempted a smile and they waited in the hall while I turned everything off and locked up. Excitement shot through me despite all my good intentions; I was going to Sadie's house – and she wasn't going to be there. Finally I had the chance to have a good poke around.

The house lights were visible from way down the street as we approached Josh's house and music spilled out into the air. I was buzzing. Fiona had been making an effort with Malika on the bus down and I left them to it, lost in my own thoughts.

The door was opened by a boy who I had never seen before. He didn't speak, just turned around and left us to shut the door behind us. This looked like my kind of party. I went straight through the house until I found the kitchen and dumped the bottle of wine I had found in Mum's cupboard on the side where it joined a mix of various bottles and cans, mostly alcoholic. Malika looked concerned. 'Take it easy, Jas, won't you?'

175

'Of course,' I said, 'stop fussing, I'm used to it.'

We found Tess and Josh in the living room, where most of the furniture had been removed and music was pumping out of a sound system which appeared to be wired throughout the whole house.

'Jasmine,' said Tess, rushing over and giving me a big hug.

'Where can I leave my stuff?' I asked. I indicated the jacket I was carrying and my clutch bag.

'Upstairs. Let me take it.'

'No, you're alright, I'll do it myself.' I took Malika's jacket too and left her with Tess. A couple were sitting on the bottom of the stairs, their lips sealed together. I clambered over them, knocking the girl in the shoulder as I went, but she didn't stir. At the top of the stairs was a room, clearly Josh's, where a couple of coats were already on the bed, obviously the cloakroom for the night. I ignored that room and carried on to the end of the corridor. There were another three doors on this level. I opened the first two, another bedroom and a toilet. The third room was hers. I opened the door and held my breath. It was a large white room, very bare, with mirrors lining one wall, tiny light bulbs around the edges, like I had seen in pictures of theatre dressing rooms. There was a double bed in the middle of the room and a large black and white photo of Sadie dominated the wall. I took out my phone and quickly took a picture of it, followed by a couple of shots of the room. A door led off the bedroom into a walk in shower room, all dark metallic tiles and steel, with a beautiful sink. Without hesitating I went straight over to the bedside cabinet. It was incredibly tidy, containing just a bottle of perfume and two magazines. I opened the small drawer underneath which contained her passport and some bank statements.

A noise outside made me jump. I closed the drawer and stood up and waited a moment. I was imagining things. Another door grabbed my attention. I opened this one and stared. I would die for this room. It was a walk in wardrobe. A room full of Sadie's clothes. My eyes were assaulted by a rainbow of colours, with boxes and boxes of shoes on a shelf above. I fingered the skirt of a silver dress, which shimmered in front of me, the fabric soft against my skin. I was just reaching up to lift another dress down, one I had seen on *Sadiestyle* and had never been able to track down, when a voice made me jump out of my skin:

'What are you doing?'

I whirled around. It was Fiona. Panic almost made me lose my balance.

'Hi,' I said lamely.

'What the hell are you up to?'

I held my hands up.

'Snooping,' I said. 'You've caught me. Thank God it was only you. I should have told you. I wanted to see if there were any clues in the house.'

'Clues. How? This is Josh's sister's room isn't it? That Sadie one who had her hands all over Khaled.'

I sighed. 'She knows him, doesn't she? So she's connected. You never know. I just thought I'd take the chance while I was here.'

My heart was pumping furiously, but she seemed to believe me.

'You're right,' she said. 'I guess this detective stuff is

177

all new to me. Have you found anything?'

I shook my head. 'Let's get out of here before anyone notices we've disappeared.'

We headed back downstairs and I cast a wistful look at Sadie's room before I closed the door, trying to etch the details into my memory. The snogging pair had moved from the stairs and were now on top of the pile of coats on Josh's bed.

'That's Tina,' said Fiona. 'She's such a tart.' The party had livened up since we arrived and people were dancing in the living room and quite a few people were outside by the pool. It was a breath taking sight. Fiona and I went to the kitchen and got some more drinks. I looked around for Tess, but couldn't see her. The kitchen was uncannily like the picture I had conjured up in my head. I was high just being in Sadie's house.

In the end I found Tess in the garden, deep in conversation with Khaled. I hoped he was making his peace with her. She saw me and waved. 'Jasmine, over here.'

'So what are you two chatting about?' I asked.

'We're friends now, aren't we Khal?' She threw her arms around him and he pushed her away. Everyone was a bit tipsy tonight, even Tess. I was feeling warm inside after my successful foray into Sadie's room and also glad to have Khaled on side.

'See you later,' he said and went back into the house.

'What did he say?' I asked.

'He apologized. He took his time getting round to it but at least I don't have to worry that he and Josh are going to get into a fight. Let's go and tell him the good news.' We made our way back to the kitchen. I glanced into the living room. Malika and Khaled were sitting on the sofa, talking. She was smiling at him and they seemed very relaxed.

The rest of the night passed in a blur. Josh had made some vivid orange punch which was sweet and gorgeous and had placed jugs of it all around the rooms downstairs. No wonder Tess was tipsy. I appropriated my own jug and lost myself in the music. The lights were dim and I danced amongst a crowd of people I didn't know, pretending I was Sadie with the copper curls. Not many people from my school were there and I relaxed and danced with abandon, not caring what I looked like.

Malika appeared at one point and asked me if I wanted to leave, but I shooed her away. Suddenly desperate for the loo, I went into the hall and stood at the bottom of the stairs, wondering how I was going to make it up to the top as the floor appeared to be shifting from under me. I could see the beige of the toilet door, but it loomed impossibly out of reach. The doorbell rang through my thoughts and I turned round and pulled the front door violently towards me.

'Welcome to the party,' I started to say, when I realised that an angry adult was standing in front of me. It was Mystery Man. He was wearing a black leather jacket and his chin was covered in dark stubble. He was enormous up close, and the look on his face made me want to get as far away from him as possible. I tried to make my legs move but my head started spinning and I vomited all over his shoes, before staggering out into the front garden.

CHAPTER 30

Malika was softly calling my name. I tried to cling onto the remnants of my dream. I couldn't remember why, but I didn't want to face the day. I groaned as pain speared behind my eyes.

'Jasmine, wake up!'

Jeez, why wouldn't she leave me alone?

'Go away.' I turned my head into the pillow.

I tried to think back to the night before. The last thing I could remember was the appearance of Mystery Man. Shocked at the recollection I tried to sit up. I managed to prop myself against the pillow. Malika was looking at me; her big eyes almost black this morning. Her hair was loosely tied back and she was wearing a pair of khakis and a grey sweatshirt. Seeing her made me feel a bit better.

'Tell me.'

'What do you remember?'

I rubbed my eyes. 'The man?'

She sighed. 'You were so sick, Jasmine, all over him. I don't even know who he was. He went into the house shouting for Josh. Tess helped me get you outside, then she went back inside to check on Josh. The man was really angry He turned the music off and sent everybody away. He must be a neighbour, or a friend of Josh's parents. Tess wanted to get you out of the

180

way so she called a cab for us. Can't you remember any of this?'

I shook my head. The last thing I could recall was Mystery Man's shoes.

'I feel terrible. Let me sleep for a couple more hours. Go down to the shop or something. I'll be alright once I've had more sleep.' I closed my eyes and turned over.

I woke feeling much better. It was twelve o'clock. I got myself into the shower and started off with ice-cold water to shock a bit of life into my body.

A noise interrupted me; it was the front door closing. Malika. I hurriedly got dressed and then made my way downstairs. Malika was sitting at the kitchen table.

'I've made you some toast,' she said, 'but there's hardly any bread.' The toast smelt good. The first slice disappeared very quickly.

'Do you feel any better?'

I nodded.

'Jasmine I wish you didn't drink. You were in a terrible state last night.'

I shrugged. 'It's not your job to worry about me.'

She looked hurt. 'I'm your sister, I can't help caring. You'd better get used to it. Besides, after what you told me about your Mum...'

'What?' The word shot out like a bullet. She looked shocked.

'Sorry, I mean...'

I sighed. 'No you're right. It's a stupid thing to do. But the way I felt last night was so awful I think I'll

181

stick to diet coke from now on.'

I finished the rest of the toast and drank the cup of tea which Malika put in front of me.

'I want to try and catch Tess and find out what happened last night.'

'After we left, you mean?'

I nodded.

Tess answered on the first ring.

'Hey Jas,' she answered. Her voice was flat, not like her usual bubbly self. 'How did you get in such a state last night? Are you OK? I was so worried.'

'Never mind that – what about Josh?' I asked. 'What happened with that man?'

'Why don't you come into town? Josh and I are in the Cyber Café. We had to get out of the house.'

'Is everything alright Tess? You sound funny.'

She sighed, 'look just get your butt over here and then I'll tell you.'

Half an hour later Malika and I walked into the café. I could see Tess's blonde curls in the far corner. She waved as she saw us approaching. Josh had his back to us. Malika went to the counter to buy some drinks. As I arrived at the table Josh turned his head to look at me. I couldn't take my eyes off his face – his eye was swollen, green and purple circles sprouting around it.

'Josh, what on earth happened?'

'You should see the other guy,' he attempted to smile but his eyes were dull.

'Josh!' Tess was indignant. 'It's not funny. Have you seen how bad your eye is?'

'Does it hurt?' Malika had just arrived at the table

and was looking distressed at the sight of Josh.

'Look sit down and stop staring at me, will you? People keep looking over.'

'Who did it?' I had a pretty good idea what the answer was going to be. 'Was it that man?'

'That man is his uncle,' said Tess, her face pink.

'He came to check up on the house. Stupidly I mentioned the party on Facebook. He must have seen it there. Old creep is far too old to be doing Facebook if you ask me. He caught me smoking a joint in the garden and went ballistic. He smacked me in the face and I fell over. I didn't even get the chance to hit him back. After that the party was pretty much killed. He turned the music off and went round yelling at everyone to get out.'

'So this uncle,' I said, 'who is he? What is he like normally?'

'He's my dad's brother, Trevor. Well, step brother, really. He didn't grow up with my dad but traced him a couple of years ago. He just showed up out of the blue one day. Dad had no idea he existed.' Malika and I looked at each other. She winked. 'Then he started coming over all the time. I've never liked him that much to be honest. Mum and Dad think he's great. I reckon there's something weird about him. You should see the way he is with Sadie.'

A cold feeling crept over me. 'What do you mean?'

'Sadie, my sister. He's kind of creepy around her. It's gross. He's always giving her presents and stuff. She liked it at first but now she can't stand him either.'

'What do you mean?'

Josh looked at me as if I was mad. 'I dunno, she

183

doesn't tell me anything.'

'Will your dad be angry with you?' Malika asked.

'He will be mad about the party, but I reckon he'll be even madder that Trevor has given me a black eye.'

'Do you know when your parents are back?' I asked.

'This evening,' groaned Josh, running his hands through his hair.

'Have you tidied up?' asked Malika, practical as ever.

Josh groaned and Tess pulled a face. 'We sort of did a bit, but we kind of ran out of steam.'

Malika looked at me. 'We could help you.'

I nodded, trying not to look too enthusiastic – it was another opportunity to have a look around Sadie's room.

'Yeah,' I said. 'We can make sure it looks perfect for when your parents come back.'

'It's got to be done,' Tess said. The four of us will get it done quicker.'

Josh nodded. 'Let's do it.' He winced as he stood up.

Malika walked ahead with Josh.

'I'm worried about him,' Tess said, as we trailed behind them. 'You should have seen that man go for him last night. I couldn't believe it when he told me he was his uncle. And what about you? Shouldn't you be lying on a bed somewhere, groaning with pain? It was a nightmare getting you home last night. I can't believe you had so much to drink.'

'Stop going on about it,' I said. 'I do feel half dead if you must know.'

We were walking briskly along and it didn't take long to get to Sadie's house.

'Hello,' Tess called out as she went in, 'anybody

184

home?'

'Tess,' I said, 'what are you doing?'

'I'm just checking,' she said. 'I don't want any nasty surprises.' She showed us the cleaning cupboard and we all set to work. Malika was already getting started on the kitchen, filling the washing up bowl with hot soapy water. Stacks of half full glasses were on every surface imaginable. There was a smell of stale smoke in the air and she opened the French doors. I went round the other rooms collecting up anything that needed washing, bringing it into the kitchen.

'I'll check upstairs,' I said. There wasn't much evidence of the party there, except in Josh's room, where a chair had been knocked over and there were still a couple of coats left on the bed. I closed the door and set off for Sadie's room. This time I wasted no time on her clothes but concentrated on the rest of the room. There was a large set of drawers which I hadn't had a chance to look at last night. The first three were full of underwear, the fourth had a couple of iPods, headphones, batteries, a torch and other random bits of uninteresting stuff, but it was the bottom drawer which got my attention. It was full of notebooks, of all different shapes and sizes. I flicked through a couple, but they were empty. Some of them had notes in; I realised they were references to shops, websites, and different items of clothing. This was probably research for her blog.

A noise made me look up. Quickly I closed the drawer and went to the top of the stairs. Malika was calling me. I ran down to the kitchen.

'How are you getting on?' she asked. She was drying

the glasses now and lining them up on the table. They actually sparkled.

'I'm almost finished. I'm going to take the hoover around the bedrooms and then I'll come back down.'

I collected the hoover and lugged it back upstairs. There were still a couple of envelopes in the drawer that I hadn't looked at. One contained a pile of tickets; I flicked through them, all gigs and theatre productions she had been to. The other was fatter and I emptied the contents onto the floor. It was a leather journal and some documents and a few photographs. I shoved the journal into my back pocket, then flicked through some old pictures of Sadie and Josh as children. The last photo had been taken on a beach, but it was cut in half. The shot was of Sadie, looking at the camera, her red hair blowing over her face, a man's leather jacketed arm around her waist. It had to be the same person. Her expression caught my attention. She almost looked frightened. I wondered who was taking the picture; whoever they were they had been cut right out. Why did she look so uncomfortable? I took out my phone and snapped the photograph.

'Jasmine!' Tess was calling me now. I jumped out of my daze and made sure the drawer was closed. I looked around the room to make sure I hadn't left anything behind. As I dragged the hoover out of the room a cute little pink silk jacket hanging on the back of the door caught my eye. It was the one Sadie had been wearing in the photo on the beach. Before I could stop myself, I whisked it off the back of the door and took it downstairs with the hoover. I made sure it was safely in my bag before I went back into the kitchen to meet

Malika.

Tess made us some tea and I lay down on the sofa, suddenly drained of energy.

'Are you alright Jas?' Tess asked as she put a mug down on the floor beside me. 'You look a bit green.'

'I think I might have overdone it a bit there.' I closed my eyes, my limbs heavy and closed my eyes. I must have slept for a while, before snippets of conversation began drifting in and out of my consciousness.

'... Mum and Dad.' Josh was speaking. 'They're really worried about her. She hasn't been herself for the past few weeks. I can't believe she's split up with AJ.'

'Would she talk to you?' Tess's voice was low.
Josh laughed. 'You're joking aren't you! What's that banging noise?'

'Malika!' Tess yelled. I opened my eyes. 'Oh, sorry Jas. But I wish your sister would sit down and stop tidying up.'

'Hmm,' I said, but my mind was elsewhere, the focus right back on Sadie again. Was she seeing someone else? Something was going on and I was curious to find out what it was. I had a feeling that somehow, all these little trails were linked together. I just needed to try and work out how.

CHAPTER 31

Malika was sitting in the kitchen, frowning at her phone.

'What's up?'

'I've just been talking to Maman. She said Papa's coming to England on Friday. He said he's going to be really busy and won't have time to see me. He's staying in a hotel.'

'Did she say which one?'

'No. She didn't seem very interested. She said she can reach him on his mobile.'

'He obviously doesn't want us to know where he's going to be – interesting don't you think?'

She looked upset. 'I don't want to believe that he's doing anything wrong.'

'Don't look like that. I've still got plenty of money left that Mum gave me for Paris. Let's book ourselves into the Metropole on Friday night – he has to be staying there, and even if he isn't we can ask around about Nora.'

My mobile started to ring.

'Hi Mum,' I said.

'Hi darling, is everything alright? I'm sorry I wasn't home to meet you, but I'll be back on Saturday.'

'That's great, Mum. I'm taking Malika to visit her aunt tomorrow.' It was kind of true. 'But we'll be back for your return and then you'll get to meet her.'

She rang off. I looked at the clock. 'I'm meeting Fiona at the park. Do you want to come?'

She pulled a face. I laughed. 'OK, I won't be long.'

Fiona was waiting for me on the swings. She wasn't scowling which was a first.

'What's up with you?' I asked.

'I copped off, didn't I? At the party. Not that you were in a fit state to notice.'

'No way! Who with?'

'Jason Bletchley. He used to be a couple of years above us. Tall, mad black hair…'

A picture popped into my mind. 'I know him,' I said. 'So does that mean you're over Khaled now?'

'Who's Khaled?' she grinned. She looked different when she smiled.

'I suppose that means you won't want to be in my detective gang any more. It's a shame because I wanted to ask your advice about some stuff, before we go away.'

'You're going away again? Where to this time?'

'To Amersham, on Friday. Malika wants to try and track down her aunt.' I filled her in on the background. 'We're going to spend a night at the hotel. I'm not sure that her aunt will be there, or even that Michael will turn up, but I promised Malika.'

'How do you know you can trust her?' asked Fiona.

'Malika? Why do you say that? She's positively saintly.'

Fiona smirked.

'Why are you looking like that?'

189

'She may come across as Little Miss Butter Won't Melt but you were so out of it at the party that you have no idea what she was up to, have you?'

'What do you mean?'

'She spent two hours talking to Khaled. Don't look like that, I timed her, for your information. Then I started talking to Jason and lost interest. But I did notice them smooching on the dance floor, just before you stole the show.'

'Malika and Khaled! I don't believe it.' *Why hadn't she said anything?*

'I didn't think you would so I took a photo. Here, look.' She clicked through the photos on her phone until she came to the right one. There was no doubt about it. Malika had her arms around Khaled. I noticed Mark was in the background looking glum. I couldn't remember him even being there. I felt a pang of guilt.

'Can you send it to me?' I asked, feeling even guiltier.

She nodded and seconds later my phone pinged. 'They're only dancing,' I pointed out, 'it doesn't mean anything.'

'Seems like you're not as close as you thought,' she said, sounding more like the Fiona I was used to. 'Jason said they definitely looked like an item.'

'What does *Jason* know?' I said, irritated now. 'He's probably just making sure you're not still lusting after Khaled. You're not are you?'

'Of course not!' she said, getting up off the bench. 'I'm with Jason now. Isn't it about time you got yourself a boyfriend, then maybe you wouldn't be so uptight? See you around.'

Malika was in the kitchen when I got back.

'I've told Mark we're going away,' I said. I'd passed him on the way in.

'Mark likes you,' Malika said, 'he spent ages yesterday asking questions about you. Why don't you want to go out with him?'

'He's Tess's brother,' I said, 'that would be so wrong. Anyway, forget me, what about you? You looked pretty friendly with Khaled at the party.'

'I just like talking to him and I danced with him because he asked me – I danced with Des, too. It doesn't mean anything.'

'Well if you talk to Khaled again then at least try and find out something more about him.'

'I have,' she said. 'He's told me all about his foster family. I like him, I don't think there's anything strange about him.'

'Did he say anything about Miriam and all that stuff?'

She shook her head. 'He's worried about something though, I can tell. He looks like he has a big heavy weight on his shoulders.'

'Probably Fiona!' I smirked, 'and you want to lift it off for him, don't you?'

She nudged me in the ribs. 'Stop teasing me.' She stretched her arms out. 'I need some fresh air. I think I'll go for a walk. Do you want to come?' I shook my head. At last I'd be able to have a look at Sadie's diary.

My heart was fluttering a little as I opened the black leather cover of the journal. It wasn't right to be looking at someone else's stuff, but what if it contained a clue?

191

Sadie's writing was bold and curly, squashed up as if she'd attempted to fit as many words on the page as possible. I was almost relieved to see that not many pages had been written on.

April 25
Dad's brother turned up last night — an uncle we had no idea existed, and neither did Dad! Trevor, that's his brother, had spent years trying to track him down and was about to contact one of those TV programmes where they help displaced families find each other again when he got lucky.

He's kind of attractive, in an old sort of way. Designer stubble, leathers, a bit rocky. AJ is really getting on my nerves lately — he desperately wants to get in to Exeter to study photography and is working all the time. He never wants to go out and I get sick of it. Camilla and Alicia's boyfriends take them out all the time. Trevor was teasing me this evening and Josh was looking at me as if I was some sort of despicable slug, but I couldn't care less what Josh thinks. He's so immature and I know it is just a laugh, a bit of fun and it has absolutely nothing to do with him. He's just as bad, always playing that stupid guitar and going on about joining a band. He'll be entering the X Factor next, and then I won't be able to show my face in public.

1000 hits on 'Sadiestyle!!! That's more than Margaret Beeston and her stupid photography site. She has so little talent I can't believe anybody ever reads it.

April 31st
Trevor turned up yesterday. I was the only one in so I made him a coffee and we had an intense conversation. He really seems to get what

I'm talking about. He asked if I'd like to go for a ride on his motorcycle! He's coming over next week.

May 5th
Trevor took me out on his bike yesterday. Wind blowing through my hair, speeding so fast and close to the ground it was amazing, like I was in a film. The best feeling ever. I think he's really nice and Mum and Dad do too. I didn't tell AJ about the ride — he doesn't like Trevor much. And I definitely won't show him the present he gave me — a lovely silver bracelet. I'd listed it on my site this week as a must have — what a coincidence!

May 7th
AJ has an essay to write and is even more unavailable than ever. Trevor asked me out for a drink — not like a date or anything, but he's so understanding. His family story is fascinating as he was brought up in care but has really done well for himself. He works in graphic design and has some really good contacts. He loves my blog, even though it's all girly stuff!

May 14th
AJ and I had a furious row this evening when I got back. He didn't like me going for a drink with Trevor. He's my uncle for God's sake!

Actually, I think Trevor likes me a bit, it's hilarious. He gave me another present tonight — a scarf. Another recommendation from Sadiestyle. I'm not going to let on I know where's he's getting his ideas from! Mum asked me if I want to invite AJ to Ibiza this summer but I'm not sure. He's getting on my nerves lately.

May 22nd
OMG, I kissed T. Why did I do that? I was kind of daring

193

myself but now I wish I hadn't. Surely he's not stupid enough to think I meant it? Afterwards I felt so guilty but I've made up for it — I told Mum I want AJ to come on holiday with us.

May 25th
I can't believe I have been so stupid — AJ was right all along. Trevor is too creepy and I don't want anything more to do with him. I wish I hadn't agree to go for dinner with him this evening but I am going to make clear to him once and for all that he must stay out of my life. I've changed my hairstyle — that will really piss him off. I wish I didn't have to go, but I'm too scared.

My fingers were like sausages as I tried to turn the page, desperate to see what came next but when I finally managed to peel the page open I let out a sigh in dismay; only a jagged edge remained where the rest of the pages had been ripped out. Why had she done that?

The front door slammed downstairs and I closed the diary and put it back in my jacket pocket and shoved it in the wardrobe. My phone pinged and I looked at the screen. Tess.

Josh's family is back tonight so I'm on my way home. Fancy a pizza later?

I wrote straight back.

Margarita with extra cheese.

I went downstairs to see if Malika wanted to come with us. She was in the kitchen with Mark, laughing at something he'd said.

'Khaled and Des are coming over tonight for band practice. Mark's invited me to watch.' Her eyes were shining. 'Will you come?'

I pulled a face. 'Tess has asked me to go out for a

pizza. I was going to invite you, but . . .'

'It's OK. I'd rather watch the band. You go out with Tess.'

So Malika would be seeing Khaled again. She certainly looked happy, maybe Fiona was right. I was glad of the opportunity to see Tess on her own – I could ask her if she'd noticed anything and hopefully get an update on Josh and his family.

CHAPTER 32

I was fifteen minutes late arriving at the pizza place. Tess waved at me from a small table towards the back of the restaurant. She stood up to give me a hug.

'Great dress!' I said. It was covered in large red poppies, with a red belt and red ballet pumps to match. Her pale face contrasted with the bright colours of the dress.

'You look tired,' I said.

She pushed a can of coke towards me.

'I've ordered already,' she said. I'd had the same favourite pizza since I was little. 'I'm so glad you could make it. I really need to talk to you about Josh.'

'Were you there when his family got home?'

She shook her head, making her curls dance on her shoulders.

'I didn't think it was a good idea. Josh had told them about the party on the phone, and his uncle and everything. But it's not just that, it's Sadie. AJ rang Josh. He said Sadie's had some sort of breakdown and they can't wait to get back home.'

'Breakdown?'

'AJ said something hasn't been right for a while. She seemed really happy that he was going on holiday with them, then told her a few days after they arrived that she was finishing with him. She's closed down her website – she runs this fashion blog thing – Josh said that is really worrying because she's got loads of followers and is so into it. She wants to be a fashion journalist, and the site is really popular.'

Strange things were happening to my insides. A kind of cold dread that Tess had no idea how much I knew about Sadie. Should I come clean? I sucked at the straw in my coke, hoping for inspiration, wishing I had never had the stupid idea to follow her round in the first place.

Tess was checking her phone. 'He's going to text me in a bit, let me know how it's going.'

A waitress appeared carrying our pizzas, and we spent the next few moments eating.

'Fiona thinks there's something going on between Malika and Khaled,' I said. 'Have you noticed anything?'

Tess opened her eyes wide. 'Really?' She thought for a moment, chewing slowly until her mouth was empty. 'They get on well, I noticed that at the party. But I was a bit tipsy, you know, not as bad as you obviously, but . . .'

'I'm giving up alcohol,' I said.

'Yeah, right.'

'No, I mean it. Malika doesn't drink and I don't want to end up like Mum.' I put my head in my hands and groaned. 'I keep thinking about that man's shoes.'

'Trevor.' Tess put her fork down. 'It was pretty spectacular. Why did he have to go and ruin the party? Josh had stopped worrying about Sadie for once and was really enjoying himself. He's so down at the moment. I hope his parents aren't too hard on him.'

We ordered ice cream for dessert and I filled Tess in on the Nora situation.

'Why wouldn't Michael tell Sara that he knew where Nora is?' I could see what Tess was thinking.

'I know. It's suspicious isn't it?' I sighed. 'I'd started to like him as well. And Sara is lovely. But I'm scared to get too close in case . . .' I couldn't put it into words. 'Malika and I are booked into the Metropole hotel tomorrow night. We reckon Michael will be staying there too, and Malika's hoping he'll lead us to Nora. I hope she isn't going to be disappointed, but I'm not convinced she'll be there.'

A beep from Tess's phone made me jump. She read the message on the screen. 'Josh wants me to ring him, I won't be long.'

By the time Tess came back in I had paid the bill and been to the ladies.

'Let's go,' she said.

The cold air hit me as we stepped outside and I wished I'd brought my jacket. We started walking in the direction of Mark's flat.

'What did he say?' I asked.

'His parents weren't too hard on him about the party — there wasn't any damage to the house after all. But his dad's furious that Trevor hit him. He's going to ring him up and tell him to stay away.'

'So is Josh feeling better about everything?'

'Well, he's relieved about the party, and that he won't have to face Trevor again. But he's still worried about Sadie.'

'What do you mean?'

'He's shocked by how awful she looks. She's lost loads of weight and barely spoke to him. His mum reckons something's happened to her, but she won't talk about it.'

Guilt hit me as I thought about the diary. Should I

mention it? But how could I explain what I'd done? I came to a decision. I'd have to investigate further, try and find some answers, then Tess would be more forgiving. My stomach was heavy as we let ourselves into the house.

CHAPTER 33

'Can I check in please?' I asked the receptionist, whose purple badge declared that her name was Elaine. Malika was flicking through a rack of leaflets on the counter.

'Is there an adult with you?'

'My dad has already arrived. Can you tell me which room he's in please?'

'What name is it?'

'Robertson, Michael Robertson.' I held my breath.

Elaine tapped the keyboard of her computer with her red nails. 'Here we are. He's in room 544,' Elaine said. 'And your room is 444. Isn't that a coincidence!' she laughed and handed me a passkey. 'Do you want me to call the room and see if he is here?'

'Actually,' I lowered my voice and leant towards her, conspiratorially. 'He doesn't know we've arrived yet and we wanted to surprise him. Would you mind keeping our arrival a secret?'

Elaine chuckled and tapped the side of her nose. 'Your secret is safe with me,' she said. 'Take the lift on the left over there and your room is just opposite.'

I thanked her and we crossed over to the lift.

'Jasmine!' Malika hissed. 'What would you have done if he wasn't here?'

'Well he is. Mum would have vouched for us anyway.

What did Sara say?'

'They've had the funeral so now she can finally relax. She's going to stay with Chantal until I come home. She says she's missing me.'

'I suppose you want to go back early now?'

'Of course not! Besides, we have work to do. Did you ask the receptionist about Nora?'

I shook my head. 'You go and ask her. I've already asked her to keep quiet about our arrival. I'll wait here.'

Malika pulled the photograph out of her bag and went over to reception. Elaine had gone behind the counter and a male receptionist had appeared in her place. I watched Malika show him the photograph. She looked across and beckoned me over. A fire lit up her eyes.

'She works here. We've found her. I can't believe it. When will she next be in?' she asked the young man, who was looking slightly bemused at her obvious excitement.

'I'll just check the rotas for you,' he said and disappeared into the office behind the counter. Malika gripped my arm, her nails pressing into my flesh.

'Ouch,' I said.

'She's using a different name but I know it's her. I won't really believe it until I see her though.'

The receptionist reappeared. 'She is next due in tomorrow morning at five. She's scheduled to start on the fifth floor.'

We thanked him and headed off for the lift. Once we were in our room Malika threw her arms around me.

'Can you believe it?' she kept saying, 'wait until I

201

tell Maman.'

'You can't say anything until we actually see her,' I said. 'I think we should stay in our room tonight. If Michael finds out we're here he might scare her away. You'll just have to be patient. We can order up a feast on room service and watch TV. I suppose you're going to make me get up at five am aren't you?'

'Stupid question,' said Malika.

It was dark. Something was digging into my shoulder. I tried to shake it off.

'Jasmine.' I could hear my name being called but I was confused. The light coming through the window was in the wrong place.

'Wake up!' A hand landed on each shoulder and dragged me awake. I remembered.

'What time is it?' I asked.

'Getting up time. We need to hurry.'

I prised my eyes open. Malika was fully dressed. 'Have you even been to bed?' I asked. 'I swear we only just turned the lights off.'

'Get up,' she insisted. I dragged my heavy body out of bed and pulled on my jeans and sweatshirt which were lying on the floor in a heap. I cleaned my teeth and splashed my face with water. I still felt half asleep.

The harsh artificial light in the corridor assaulted my eyes as soon as Malika opened the door. The corridor was eerily silent apart from the faint buzzing of the lights. There wasn't a soul in sight. Malika pointed to the ceiling. Floor five awaited. We took the lift and I turned my back on the mirrored wall inside, horrified by the quick glimpse I had of myself, hair sticking up all over the place. Malika looked normal, black scarf in place, clothes neat, as if she always got up at this time of the morning. She looked scared though, her mouth pinched and her eyes giving her anxiety away. The lift door slid open and we stepped out onto an identical floor from which we had come. There was a rattling sound and a cleaner with a trolley appeared at the other end of the corridor.

'Is it her?' I whispered. Malika shook her head and strode off towards the woman who was filling her arms with supplies from the trolley.

'I no speak English,' I heard the woman say. Malika held out the photograph. The woman looked at it for a long moment. She looked suspicious. 'Why you want her? No trouble?'

'She's my aunt,' Malika said. The woman relaxed and pointed to one of the rooms. Malika's body went rigid and she put her hand to her mouth.

'Come on,' I said, taking hold of her arm. 'Thanks,' I said to the woman who was staring at Malika. I dragged her out into the corridor. Outside the room next door Malika hesitated.

'I'm scared,' she said.

'I'm right behind you,' I said and pushed her into the room.

CHAPTER 34

Another woman dressed in a blue overall was folding towels up, her back to us. I prodded Malika but she remained frozen.

'Hello,' I said. The woman turned around, as if expecting company. Malika stepped forward.

'Nora? It's me, Malika, your niece.'

The woman stared at her for a moment, before a look of astonishment crossed her face, quickly replaced by delight. She let out a sort of squeal and threw her arms around Malika. They stayed like that for what seemed like ages, both sobbing. Eventually Nora drew backwards, holding Malika at arms length, looking into her eyes.

'You are the image of your mother as a child. How did you find me?'

Malika's mouth was moving but she couldn't seem to speak. I stepped forward.

'I'm Jasmine. I think she's in shock.'

'Aunty Nora. I've found you at last. I can't believe it.'

Nora's delight was transforming into something else. She rubbed her hands over and over.

'How did you find me? I don't use the name Nora here. Have you told the hotel I am not who they think? I need this job.'

Malika rattled something off in French. They spoke for a few minutes and then hugged each other again. Malika turned to me. 'She's going to come to our room after her shift has finished. It will be about nine o'clock.' She turned and looked at her aunt again. 'You promised me,' she said. 'I never want to lose you again.' They embraced again and Nora pulled out a large tissue and wiped her eyes.

'I will be there.'

Malika and I went down in the lift in silence.

'Let's have breakfast,' I said, suddenly ravenous.

'What about Papa?'

'No way will he get up this early. Please, I'm starving.'

A grin transformed her face. 'Me too,' she said.

The breakfast was a buffet and I decided to try and have a piece of every single thing on the menu. Malika rolled her eyes at me and took some toast and a cup of tea. I had got through two cups of hot chocolate, cereal, a round of toast and jam, and was just starting on a chocolate croissant when Malika suddenly looked horrified.

'Don't look round,' she said, 'it's Papa. He's got his back to us. Quick, we can get out here.' She indicated the exit to her left. We rushed out of the door. I managed to hold on to my croissant. We didn't bother with the lift but took the stairs two at a time, haring down the corridor to our room. Once safely inside we collapsed on the bed, panting heavily.

'That was close,' I said.

'We didn't clear up the table,' said Malika, looking worried. 'They will think we are very rude.

'It was an emergency,' I said, stuffing the remnants of the croissant in my mouth, 'it couldn't be helped. 'I'm going back to sleep. Wake me in an hour.'

I heard Malika starting the water in the shower and I lay still, waiting for my heartbeat to return to normal. I didn't sleep for long and got into the shower myself to freshen up before Nora's visit.

'Do you think she will turn up?' I asked when there was a rap at the door. Malika hesitated, then went and opened it. She came back into the room followed by her aunt. Nora ignored the armchair, perching instead on the edge of a hard backed chair close to the door, as if ready to flee at any moment.

'Speak in English,' Malika said.

'How did you find me?' she said, her French accent was very strong.

'Jasmine found you. Jasmine is my half-sister. We only just found out about each other.'

'Caroline's daughter,' said Nora, 'I can see the likeness.'

'You know my mother?' I asked. She shook her head.

'I've seen a photo.'

'Dad's mother is ill and Caroline called to tell him,' continued Malika. 'Jasmine found out he'd been in England and she wanted to know what he was doing here. He's been very strange, Nora, he didn't tell us he was in England. He went to visit his mother and left your photograph there. Jasmine saw your photo and assumed it was Maman. When she showed me the photograph I knew straight away it was you and that it was a recent photo, which meant that you were alive.

Why did you disappear like that? I was so afraid you were dead.' She wiped her eyes. 'I have some bad news for you.'

Nora sat down on the bed.

'Not Sara?' she whispered, her eyes large and filled with fear.

Malika knelt down beside her and took her hands.

'No. You must prepare yourself. It's your brother. Ali has died.'

A strange sound escaped from Nora's mouth and her skin went a strange colour. 'Ali, dead? Really, are you sure?'

'I'm sorry to tell you so suddenly but I thought you would want to know. It only happened last week. Mum has gone to stay in Lille. I know you were very close. I'm sorry to make you sad.'

Nora stood up and went over to the window. She gazed outside for what seemed like a long time. Then she came back over to us, shaking her head.

'You aren't making me sad mon enfant, quite the opposite. For the first time in years I am happy.'

'What do you mean?' asked Malika.

Nora remained silent, staring out of the window. At last she turned around to face us.

'Ali is the reason I left France,' she said, sighing.

'What do you mean?' Malika said, sitting down on the floor.

Nora nodded, 'I think you are old enough to hear the truth. When I was sixteen I had a boyfriend and I became pregnant. My parents knew nothing about my relationship and when they found out they were horrified. Ali in particular took the news badly. He was

207

angry when he found out and he hit me so hard, I was afraid that I had lost the baby. He wouldn't leave me alone after that, he was constantly taunting me about the shame I had brought upon the family. I was so young, and I was terrified, but I couldn't bear to give up my baby. Ali swore that if I gave birth he would kill the child. I couldn't stay in the same house as that monster any longer so I ran away. I ran as far as I could and ended up here in England.'

'Mum would have understood, why didn't you come and live with us?'

She smiled sadly. 'I know that now but at the time I believed my mother when she said I was disgracing the whole family. Sara was pregnant with you and I was scared that if she knew where I was Ali would be able to find me.'

'Your mother went back to Morocco shortly after that.'

'I know, I heard.'

'From Michael?' I asked. She nodded.

'I don't understand, why does Papa know about you? Has he always known? How could you tell him and not Maman?'

'It wasn't like that. I only got in touch with him recently. I had a problem that I needed help with. Michael was the only person I could think of to help me.'

'What problem. . ?' Malika started to say, the words drying up in her mouth as somebody started banging loudly on the door. We all looked at each other, frozen with shock.

'Open the door! I know you're in there.' Michael's

voice sliced into the room. Nora stood up and went slowly towards the door.

'I'll let him in,' she said. I turned to Malika.

'You know what this means?' I said, relief flooding through me. She looked at me, her eyes shining and nodded. 'Michael had a reason to be here. Maybe he had nothing to do with Miriam after all.'

CHAPTER 35

Nora opened the door to reveal Michael standing in the doorway. He charged into the room.

'What the hell is going on?' he asked. 'What are you girls doing here? Why aren't you in London?'

'It was a surprise,' I said. 'We thought you would be pleased.' I tried to smile at him but my mouth wasn't moving properly.

'Nora, tell me what is going on here? How have they found you?'

Malika stood up. She went and stood behind her aunt's chair and launched into a passionate speech in French. The words battered my ears and I wished I'd paid more attention in French lessons. At the end she burst into tears and her aunt pulled her onto her lap and started shouting at Michael.

'Hello?' I said, but Michael stood still, like stone.

'Michael,' Nora said. 'It's all out in the open now. It's probably for the best.'

'Excuse me,' I said, 'I don't speak French. Can someone tell me what's going on? Why have you been meeting Nora in secret? How could you do this to Sara and Malika?'

Michael sank down onto the couch. 'Nora was in trouble. She contacted me and asked me to help her. She swore me to secrecy. I can't tell you any more than that at the moment.'

'Was it to do with Gran? Is that why you went to see her?'

He sighed. 'No, I just took the opportunity to visit her. I was hoping she'd let me back into her life now that we're moving back to England. I showed her a photo of Malika, I was hoping she'd want to see her, but it just made her angry.'

'So after you saw Gran, did you come back here, to this hotel, to see Nora?'

He nodded. 'It was Malika's birthday, and I felt terrible about missing that, but Nora needed to see me. We went out for dinner. I'm sorry I can't tell you more, I have to respect Nora's wishes.'

'I forgive you, now that Nora is back. I can't wait to tell Maman,' said Malika. 'She will be so happy.' She looked at her aunt. 'She never gave up hoping you would come back, you know?'

Malika was a lot more forgiving than me. They were still keeping secrets from us.

Nora stroked Malika's hair. 'I believe you, chérie, but I want you to promise me one thing. Not a word to Sara.'

'But…' Malika sat up in protest.

'I want to be the one to tell her. You must understand that.'

'So what happened to your child?' I asked. 'Did you have it?'

She nodded. 'A boy.'

'He's my cousin,' Malika laughed. 'Can I see him?'

A sad expression crossed her eyes. 'He isn't here at the moment. Maybe another time.'

Malika and I couldn't stop talking on the way back to London. Michael was staying in Buckinghamshire for a couple of days more.

'Did you think Nora was a bit funny about her son?' Malika asked. 'She didn't seem to want to talk about him.'

I nodded. 'I reckon this secret that Michael isn't telling us has something to do with him. But at least he has an alibi.' Malika had quizzed Nora on the meal she'd had with Michael, and they'd been together all evening.

'I still don't get why he left the scene of the crime. I think I'll just have to ask him about it, tell him about *Crimewatch*. Otherwise I will always be wondering whether he had anything to do with Miriam's death or not.'

Tess was pleased we were back.

'I've persuaded Josh to have everyone over to his place tomorrow night – I'm hoping it will cheer him up. The band has got some stuff to talk about and Mark suggested you bring Malika. Come about seven, OK?'

I went upstairs to my bedroom to have a rest before going out later. Malika was watching TV downstairs. As I hung my bag up in the wardrobe, a flash of pink caught my eye. It was Sadie's jacket; I had forgotten all about it. I took it out of the wardrobe; despite having been scrunched up the material fell beautifully into place and was exquisitely soft to touch. I couldn't resist putting it on. I looked at myself in the mirror, shoving my left hand in the pockets as I did so. A wodge of paper was in the pocket and I drew it out, curious. My stomach did a somersault. I knew straight away what it was. It was the missing pages from the diary. I made sure my bedroom door was shut and I sat on the floor, unfolded the papers and started reading.

I went to the restaurant last night as arranged with Trevor. I deliberately wore my jeans and a jumper and he had a go at me for not dressing up. I said to him he sounded like he thought we were on a date and he said that of course we were. I told him not to be silly, then came out with my speech — how he had been really good to me, giving me presents and stuff but I was worried he had got the wrong idea. I told him when I kissed him that one time it was my idea of a joke — he knew I was going out with AJ after all. His eyes kind of bulged when I said that and that's when I began to feel uneasy. I was right to be because then he told me that he had booked a room upstairs in the hotel. That really scared me. I couldn't believe I had been so stupid. How could he think I would ever go out with him — he is so old, apart from being my half uncle. I pretended to go to the toilet but I went to reception and asked the lady there to book me a taxi. When the cab came I asked her to wait five minutes, then send a message through to Trevor that I had been taken ill and gone home. I spent the whole journey back watching the mirror, terrified that Trevor would try to follow. I was so relieved when the cab made it home and even more so when I ran into one of Josh's friends just outside my house. I couldn't hide how upset I was and burst into tears. I ended up telling him everything. We went for a long walk, then a coffee, before he walked me home. It was gone three when I finally went to bed. He helped calm me down and I made him promise not to say anything. I couldn't tell Mum and Dad, they think Trevor can do no wrong. I am so glad we are going on holiday next week. I hope I never have to see that man again.

The pages came to an abrupt end. She must have taken them to stop anyone finding them. I stood up and paced around in circles; I couldn't believe what I had just read. I realised I was still wearing the jacket, and put my hands back into the pockets, hoping there might be a few more pages. I hadn't checked the right pocket and I thrust my hand inside, only to find another piece of paper. The paper was thicker; it was a photograph – the missing half of the beach photo to be precise, with something written on the back. A man had his arm around Sadie, his leather jacket on the edge of the shot as he awkwardly held the camera at arm's length to take the picture. With a jolt I found myself looking into Mystery Man's eyes. *Trevor*, I reminded myself. I turned the photograph over, '*Me and my girl*' it said.

If Khaled was the friend that Sadie had run into, this would explain how they knew one another and why he wouldn't tell Fiona how he knew Sadie. I went to the wardrobe and took the diary out of my pocket. My hands were trembling as I turned to the extract before the pages had been removed. I needed to know what date this had been written on. The words burned into my eyes. May 25th. The day Miriam had been attacked. If I was right, then I was holding Khaled's alibi. But how on earth could I use it, without betraying Sadie?

CHAPTER 36

'Jasmine, is that you?' Mum's voice rang out as I stepped into the hall. Malika looked at me, raising her eyebrows. I hoped my smile was reassuring.

I went into the room. Mum was sitting at the table, drinking a cup of coffee.

'Darling,' she said. 'I've missed you.'

'I bet you have,' I said, as I went and gave her a hug. She was looking quizzically at Malika. 'This is Malika, remember?'

'Oh yes,' she said. 'I'm not likely to forget your *sister* am I?' I gave her a warning glance. She held out her hand to Malika. 'I've literally just got back,' she said, sweeping her hand out with a flourish to indicate the bags dumped at her feet. 'I know we've got loads to talk about and I want to hear all about you,' she said to Malika, 'but I'm dying for a long soak in the bath. I expect you girls have got plenty to do as it is, so let's catch up later.' She eased herself gently off the coach, wincing as if in pain. 'It's jet lag,' she said to Malika, 'a long flight and not much sleep. I'll be fabulous company this evening, I promise you. Let's go out to dinner.'

'We can't Mum, Josh has invited us over.'

'Josh?'

'Tess's boyfriend.'

Mum raised her eyebrows.

'I can see a lot has been going on in my absence. Are you going out with that, whatshisname, Karl yet?'

'Mum!' I said. 'Go and have your bath.'

She stopped for a moment, staring at Malika. A pained look flittered across her face.

'You do look a bit like Michael,' she said. With that she disappeared off upstairs.

Malika looked puzzled. 'This is very strange, how you live here. Is it always like this?'

'Pretty much,' I said, 'I tried to warn you.'

'I guess I didn't want to believe you.'

Footsteps sounded overhead and the boiler in the kitchen started spluttering and gurgling.

'She'll be in there for at least an hour,' I said, 'then she'll be on the phone to Clare. I bet we won't see her again this evening.'

Malika rang Josh's doorbell and we stood back and waited. I felt a trickle of dread run through me; I couldn't quite believe what I had read this afternoon. The more I found out about Sadie the more shallow I felt for getting involved in her life. Guilt about taking the diary was eating me up. I still didn't know what to do about it; it sat like a stone in my bag at the moment, along with the pink silk jacket.

Josh opened the front door. The colours around his eye were muted, less obvious. 'Cheers for tidying up the other day,' he said.

'I'm glad your dad has got rid of that Trevor,' I said.

'He turned up again, you know, even after Dad rang him – I thought they were going to have a massive bust up. He screeched off on that stupid bike of his. I hope we never see him again. My sister's mad as well because she reckons he was rooting around in her things. I don't know whether he would do that kind of thing though – I hope it wasn't anyone at the party.'

A cold chill trickled slowly through my veins. The name Trevor made me feel sick. Since I had read Sadie's diary she had become real to me, a person with feelings and worries. What was I thinking, following her around like that, copying her? She didn't have the perfect life that I thought she had. Now I knew stuff about her that I wished I didn't and no way could I tell anyone. There and then I made up my mind to put the diary back. It was bad enough Trevor pursuing her. Wasn't I just as bad?

Josh led us into the sitting room, where everyone was sitting on the floor. Beers and cokes were lined up on the table. I stared at the cans, memories of the party flashing through my head. I took two cans of coke and handed one to Malika. She smiled. Tess was selecting some music on the iPod and Khaled and Des were chatting about their last rehearsal.

'Are your mum and dad home?' I asked Josh.

'They've gone to the cinema. Sadie's out but she'll be back soon.'

Malika sat down next to Khaled.

'I'll be back in a minute,' I said, 'I need the bathroom.' I took the stairs two at a time.

Sadie's door was closed. Even though I knew she was out, my heartbeat rose at the fear of being caught in the act. Supposing Josh was mistaken? This was no time to mess about. I pushed the door carefully and it

217

swung open to reveal an empty room. I paused, listening. There was no sound from the bathroom either. I could feel the eyes on the large photo of Sadie watching me, following me around the room, judging me. Wasting no time I went straight to the drawer and put the notebook back where I had found it. I hung the jacket back on the door, making sure the papers were where I left them. As I shut the door I wondered if I would ever be able to put Sadie behind me. I squirmed with shame at the thought of how I'd behaved.

A sound like that of the front door shutting caught my ears. I rushed out of the room, closing the door quickly behind me. I went into the bathroom and splashed my face with cold water. The sound of a muffled conversation pricked my attention. I closed the door softly, then made sure it was locked, as footsteps came up the stairs. My breath caught in my throat as I recognized Khaled's voice. He was talking to Sadie. There was a shuffling noise and the stairs creaked. It sounded as if they were sitting at the top of the stairs.

'You don't look well,' he said. 'What's going on? Did you tell AJ what happened that night?'

'I couldn't,' she said. She was speaking so softly it was difficult to hear her. 'I felt so guilty. It was all my fault for leading him on. AJ would have chucked me anyway, so I made it easy for him.'

'But he's in bits! He hasn't got a clue what's going on. And how is any of that your fault? Trevor threatened you. Has he been in touch since?'

She must have nodded. 'He started contacting me through my website. That's why I had to close it down. All those stupid presents – I thought it was flattering at first, that he was finding out what I liked from my blog, but then it just got creepy, he wouldn't leave me alone.'

'So why not tell your parents? Or at least AJ?'

'Because I'm scared.'

'Of what? What can he do now? Your parents know what he's like.'

There was a long silence.

'Sadie?'

'If I tell you will you promise not to tell anyone.'

'Yeah.'

'I can't tell AJ because he'd want to have it out with Trevor, And I don't want that to happen because I think Trevor is dangerous. I'm scared of what he might do, what he might have done.'

'What do you mean?'

Sadie's voice cracked and she started to cry.

'Haven't you worked it out? Trevor lives in Keston. I've seen his house. He took me there once on his bike. That night, that girl, Miriam. He would have been so angry with me. I think he killed her.'

I was unable to breathe.

A shout from downstairs interrupted the strained silence that had descended. 'Khaled! Where are you?'

'Coming!' he replied. Sadie spoke again but I couldn't catch what she said. I listened as Khaled ran down the stairs and waited for Sadie's door to close. I lingered a few more minutes before I eased the bathroom door open and slipped down the stairs as fast as I could.

Back downstairs I went into the living room and picked

up my drink. Malika was telling the group about her life in France. My heart was banging so hard I was convinced the others would be able to hear it.

'Have you got a boyfriend back home?' Tess asked.

Malika laughed and shook her head. 'Nobody special.' Out of the corner of my eye I noticed Josh dig Des in the ribs. Maybe Fiona was right.

'Where's Fiona?' I asked.

Tess rolled her eyes. 'She's totally loved up with her new boyfriend. She's so over you,' she said to Khaled. 'I suppose you want her back now, don't you?'

Khaled was standing over by the window, his arms hanging at his sides, his fists clenched.

'Who wants another drink?' Josh asked.

'I'll get them,' I said. I went back into the kitchen and was standing in front of the fridge thinking how strange it was that I should be standing in Sadie's kitchen when the door opened and then she was there in front of me. The ruby red lips were gone, the extensions no more, and she was a lot thinner. Her eyes were expressionless, the sparkle lost. She stared at me.

'I'm Josh's friend,' I said, 'well a friend of his girlfriend, Tess, really.'

'Whatever,' she said, looking at me as if I was some sort of specimen, before going to the sink and pouring herself a glass of water. Then she went back upstairs, pulling the door shut behind her.

I stood motionless, gazing at the closed door. I imagined calling her back, explaining, apologising for intruding into her life. I shook my head; I couldn't do it. Clearly I meant nothing to her.

Tess and I went to sit in the garden for a bit. A cool

breeze was blowing through the trees.

'You'll have to go back home soon,' I said. 'Will you carry on going out with Josh?'

She nodded. 'I've only got one more year of school, then I'm definitely moving back here. Mum will be fine with it; she just wants me to finish my GCSE's at the same school. I'd be going to a sixth form college anyway, so it doesn't matter where it is. And she's happy that I can stay with Mark, he's very sensible. Talking of sensible, isn't that just what you need?'

'Get lost,' I said. 'I've got far too much to think about at the moment.' I told her what had happened at the hotel.

'So Michael's in the clear?' she asked. I nodded. 'I think so, although I still don't know why he would leave the scene of the crime like that and there's still something he and Nora aren't telling us, I'm sure of it. I've decided I'm just going to be upfront about it and ask him.'

'At least that way you'll know one way or another.'

We were silent for a bit, listening to the sounds of murmured conversation and music coming from inside.

'Tess,' I said. She looked at me. 'I'm glad you're coming back. I lost it a bit when you left, you know? First Gran, then you,' I held my can of coke against my forehead; it was cool, soothing the thoughts that were burning inside.

'I know.' I looked at her in surprise. 'Your Mum rang my mum – don't look at me like that Jas, she was really concerned about you. I was too, but they thought it would make it worse if I kept ringing you when you were trying to get used to me being away and made me stop calling for a bit.'

I shook my head. 'I can't believe it,' I said. 'I thought you were turning against me too.' I took a deep breath. 'That's when I did something stupid.'

'What do you mean?'

I took a long swig of my drink before I spoke.

'I latched onto Sadie.'

She turned to look at me. 'Sadie? Josh's Sadie?'

I nodded. 'She just happened to be in the wrong place at the wrong time and I thought it would be fun to find out about her, but I kind of got obsessed. I thought she was the answer to all my prayers. If I copied her, looked like her, I would feel better about myself and people would like me. It didn't happen – no surprises there.' It was hard to look at her. 'This is so embarrassing.'

Tess's forehead was crinkled up in astonishment. 'The red hair! You're not still…'

'No! But I wanted you to know. It's funny but since I met Malika I started losing interest.'

'You're not getting obsessed with her are you?'

'No!'

'That's a relief. I can't imagine you in a headscarf.'

'Idiot! Promise me you'll never tell anyone, especially Josh.'

She pulled an imaginary zip across her lips. 'You can count on Tess.'

She was right. I'd always known I could trust her. I could tell her everything. She'd know what to do about Sadie and Trevor and Khaled.

'Talking of Sadie,' I began, when Josh appeared at the back door.

'Tess!' he called.

A smile lit up her face. 'One minute,' she yelled, 'What is it?' she asked, turning back to me.

She looked radiant, the yellow light picking out the blonde of her hair.

'It's nothing,' I said, 'Go to lover boy.'

She stuck her arm through mine and we made our way back to the house. I hesitated when I got to the back porch. Through the window I could see Malika engrossed in conversation with Khaled. He left the room as I made my way across to her.

'What were you and Khaled talking about?'

'About his foster family again. His Mum was in some sort of trouble and couldn't look after him, but the family he is with now are good to him. I think he's a bit spoilt, but in a good way.'

'Maybe I should find myself a foster family,' I said, 'Mum would like that, I bet.'

'Don't talk like that,' she said, 'I thought you were starting to believe that Papa is innocent.'

I sighed. 'Yes, I am. But why would he run away from the police? I'm scared to ask him, in case I don't like the answer. Then I would lose him all over again.'

I looked into her eyes, Michael's eyes, eyes that looked like mine. I still couldn't get used to it.

'Well whatever happens,' she said, 'you've got me now, and I'm not letting you go anywhere.'

CHAPTER 37

It was about ten o'clock when we got home. The hall light was on – I hoped Mum was awake and not passed out on the sofa again. I put my key in the door and as I did so I heard the sound of voices. I stood on the doorstep for a moment, preparing myself. I wasn't in the mood for one of her friends. Mum's voice was raised and a deep masculine voice murmured in response.

'Papa,' shouted Malika, and pushed past me. I was horrified. What was he doing here? I took a deep breath, thankful that I'd stuck to the coke, and went into the room.

Mum was perched on the edge of the sofa, the inevitable glass of wine in her hand. Michael was standing by the window, leaning against the wall. The atmosphere was strained. Malika ran over to him and threw herself into his arms for a big bear hug. I looked away.

'Hello Jasmine,' he said.

I turned to Mum.

'Why is he here? You always said you would kill him if he ever came near you again and he looks pretty much alive to me.'

'Jasmine!' she tutted. I went into the kitchen and

opened the fridge. I gazed at the bottle of vodka, just for a second, but I went for the coke instead and took my time adding three large ice cubes to the glass. It was cool to the touch. A little calmer, I headed back to the parental war zone.

'So what's going on?' I asked.

'You explain,' said Mum to Michael.

'I thought it was about time your mother and I had a talk.'

'It's a bit late for that isn't it? Like about fourteen years late?' The words twisted out of my mouth.

Mum sighed dramatically. 'Let him speak, for goodness' sake. I've had enough of all this arguing.'

I glared at Mum. Michael cleared his throat.

'As I was saying, I phoned Caroline and she suggested coming over. It was great getting to know you in Paris, not just for me but Malika and Sara too. Now that we're going to be living in the same country I wanted to check with Caroline how she felt about us all staying in touch. I know I've behaved terribly in the past and I didn't want to repeat the same mistakes again.'

I looked at Mum, she was composed, and she didn't look angry.

'So, is this alright with you Mum?' I asked. Malika had been standing over by the window during this exchange. She crossed the room and sat down next to Mum. She leant over and squeezed my arm.

'If you'd phoned me a week ago Michael, suggesting you came over I would have told you where to go in no uncertain terms. But now that I've met Malika,' she broke off to pat her on the arm, 'I can see how well you girls get on and I don't want to stand in your way. It doesn't mean your Dad and I are now best friends again, God forbid,' she added, grimacing at Michael. 'But if you want to go and stay in Buckinghamshire that's fine by me and Malika is always welcome here.'

'She might not be coming to see me,' I said. 'Malika's got herself a boyfriend here.'

'No I haven't,' said Malika, frowning.

'Is this true?' asked Michael.

'Don't be shy,' I said, 'they don't stop talking every time they see each other. He's in Mark's band. You met him once Mum, remember, he came here when I was in France. Khaled.'

Mum and Michael were staring at one another. A strange silence settled into the room.   Michael had gone very pale. 'Did you say Khaled?' he asked.

'Yes, Khaled Hussein. You can't possibly know him.'

Mum stood up and went out of the room. She came back with a full glass of wine. She wobbled a little as she sat back down on the sofa.

'You'll have to tell them Michael, this can't be allowed to happen.'

'Papa, what is it?' Malika asked.

Michael slumped down in the armchair and put his head in his hands.

'For God's sake, Michael, just spit it out,' Mum said. She swivelled on the sofa to make eye contact with Malika. 'You can't go out with Khaled, Malika, because he's your cousin.'

Malika gasped, speechless.

'He's Nora's child,' Michael said, his voice sounding grave. 'The child she was telling you about. That's why

226

she got in touch with me and asked me to come up to see her. Khaled had got himself into trouble and she needed help. She placed him in foster care because she couldn't cope with him on her own, but he's still in touch with her.'

As he spoke, more fragments turned into pieces, clunking loudly as they fell one by one into place.

'I know why you had to come over,' I said. 'Nora knew he was going out with Miriam. She asked for your advice, and then her body was found. You thought Khaled had killed her.'

The four of us looked at one another. It felt like a scene from a play, only I wasn't quite sure of my lines. Mum picked up the cue.

'What are you talking about?'

I picked up my bag and extricated the newspaper cutting I'd kept in there since I'd first read it. I handed it over to Michael. His face went white when he recognized himself in the photofit. His eyes scanned the article and he collapsed onto a chair.

'Did you think I was guilty?' I bit down hard on my lip. 'How could you possibly think I was a murderer?' he asked, his face creased into a picture of disbelief, his eyes boring into me. I looked directly back at him.

'How would I know otherwise?' I said quietly.

Malika spoke in my defence. 'Papa, I have known you all my life and I couldn't understand why you would have left the scene of a crime. Then I discovered that you had been in touch with Aunt Nora who had also disappeared…'

'OK, OK,' Michael said, 'I see.'

'So tell us why you didn't stay and wait for the

227

police. Was it because you thought Khaled had done it?'

'I had never met the boy at that point and I had no idea whether he was guilty or not, but your aunt was in a terrible state. She knew Khaled had been going out with Miriam and she was worried that Miriam was so young. She wanted me to have a chat with him. Then when Miriam was killed,' he paused, running his hands through his hair, 'Yes I was afraid that Khaled was involved. I hadn't even met him, remember. I thought that if the police looked into my family they would link me to Nora and find Khaled and I panicked. I couldn't put Nora through that.'

'But it would have been wrong, Dad, if he was guilty.'

'I know, I know.'

'So how do you know Khaled isn't guilty?' asked Mum.

Michael put his head in his hands. 'I don't,' he said, his words sounding strangled.

'What I want to know,' Mum said suddenly, 'is how did I miss all this? How did I not see Michael on Crimewatch, or in the newspapers?'

'Because you're always working, Mum,' I said. 'You never have time to do anything else. When did you last watch TV? You make it easy for me to keep things secret.'

Michael yawned and rubbed his eyes. 'Look, it's getting late. I need to get off.'

He looked different now that I knew he was innocent; vulnerable, human, a person who could make mistakes.

'Can't he stay here Mum?' The words surprised me as they tumbled out of my mouth.

'You'll have to sleep on the sofa,' she said, 'Malika's in the spare room.'

'A sofa sounds heavenly right at this minute,' he said, 'especially when my oldest daughter has offered it to me.'

'Yeah, well, don't get too excited,' I said, embarrassed, 'it's only a sofa.'

We all went to bed after that. I had just snuggled under my duvet when there was a light tap at the door. Malika came in and lay down next to me on the bed.

'Are you alright?' I asked, 'finding out about Khaled I mean?'

'Of course I am,' she said. 'Who told you about me and Khaled?'

'Fiona,' I said.

'Exactly. Fiona exaggerates everything and she is jealous. Khaled and I get on really well, just like you and I do. I reckon it must be a family thing. I knew there was something familiar about him. I'm glad he's my cousin – family is the most important thing to me.'

'Good job,' I said, 'it seems to be getting bigger every day!'

'I'm going to go and see him tomorrow, tell him I know everything. No wonder he's in such a state.'

She went to bed after that but I was awake for ages, not sleeping, thoughts going round and round in my head. At about two in the morning I logged onto my computer and deleted all the folders I had compiled on Sadie. I didn't need her anymore; I was finally starting to work out who I was.

229

CHAPTER 38

Michael was up when I went downstairs the next morning. He was finishing a call on his mobile when I went into the room.

'The police,' he said, 'I'm going in to see them this morning. I want to get myself removed from Britain's most wanted top ten. How about while I make some coffee you log on to this *Crimewatch* site?' He shook his head. 'I still can't believe that. I want to see the evidence for myself.'

I sat down at Mum's desk and booted up her computer. The aroma of fresh coffee soon wafted into the room, waking me up. Michael put a cup down in front of me.

'Thanks,' I said. It felt good, drinking coffee together, just me and him, the rest of the house asleep.

I opened the *Crimewatch* gallery. Michael gasped aloud when he saw his picture.

'It is me!' he said, 'I didn't quite believe it would be, but...yeah, that's when I was waiting for the policeman to come, just before I changed my mind. I can't believe you recognised me after all this time.' He shook his head in disbelief.

'I used to look at your pictures every day. I wanted to memorise your face in case I ever saw you one day. I didn't realise it would be quite like this.'

We were both quiet with our thoughts for a moment. Michael broke the silence. 'Let's look at the rest of the case report; I want to read the whole thing.'

I clicked back to the home page. It would probably be old news now and take ages to find. I was shocked when a headline flashed up:

ARREST MADE IN MIRIAM JACKSON CASE

'Look!' I said, pointing to the headline. I felt sick. 'Do you think they've arrested Khaled?'

The headline was large and bold:

ARRESTED MAN CONFESSES ALL – TREVOR THOMSON HELD IN MIRIAM CASE

Underneath there was a photo of the man I had last seen storming into Josh's house. I gasped.

'What is it?' asked Michael. He sat down next to me and peered over my shoulder.

'Read it to me,' he said.

A man was arrested last night in connection with the disappearance and murder of Miriam Jackson, 13. Trevor Thomson 40, a builder was stopped by police at 11.15pm last night after he was spotted driving erratically on a dual carriageway. Thomson, 40, was breathalysed by police and found to be considerably over the limit. He was taken to the local police station, where he confessed to police that he had abducted and strangled Miriam Jackson on May 25th earlier this year. Thomson allegedly told officers that he had been upset as a result of an argument with his girlfriend and gone to a local bar where he

231

had consumed several drinks before heading back to his car. Passing the station he had come across Miriam and he had offered her a lift home. When she refused, he attacked her and left her in the nearby woodland. Thomson remains in police custody while police continue with their enquiries.

I swallowed hard, my throat dry. Khaled didn't need Sadie to give him an alibi now. Her secret was safe. I was relieved. It was hers to tell after all, if she chose to, and it was none of my business. Sadie was none of my business. I had my own family now. My eyes started prickling.

'Are you OK?' asked Michael.

I shook my head. 'It's so sad, what happened to her and I feel bad for not trusting you. How could I possibly have thought you were guilty?'

'Well you did see me on *Crimewatch*. I'm glad you did what you did.'

'Why?' I asked.

'Because it brought us together. You wouldn't have come to stay otherwise, would you?'

I shook my head slowly.

'There you go. Now how about we finish our breakfast and we can go down to the police station afterwards?'

I looked him square in the face. I hadn't noticed before how kind his eyes were. Kind, like my sister's.

I thought about it. Maybe having a Dad who was wanted on *Crimewatch* was quite cool after all. Especially when he was innocent.

'You're on,' I said, 'but only if you let me have the last piece of toast.'

ACKNOWLEDGEMENTS

I would like to thank the following people for their support and encouragement, helping to make this book possible:

Paul Cheetham, Ella Ruth Cowperthwaite, Tanita Alethiea Gibbs, Rosanna Mclaughlin, Sabah Mohamed, , Nariece Sanderson, Sabrina Sattaur and Julie Sparks.

ABOUT THE AUTHOR

Lesley Cheetham is a secondary school librarian in London. She studied French and Theatre Studies at Warwick University. She lives in King's Cross with her husband. In her spare time she enjoys reading, writing, swimming, running and languages. *Someone Like Me* is her third novel for teenagers.

www.lesleycheetham.com

Published by LambChop Publishing, London 2014

A catalogue record for this book is available from the British Library

ISBN 13: 978-0957285828

ISBN 10: 0957285825

ISLINGTON

Please return this item on or before the last date stamped below or you may be liable to overdue charges. To renew an item call the number below, or access the online catalogue at www.islington.gov.uk/libraries. You will need your library membership number and PIN number.

4/14

Islington Libraries

020 7527 6900   **www.islington.gov.uk/libraries**

LambChop publishing WC1